ISBN-13: 9781096761525

Non-Fiction Books by Maureen Wood (writing with Ron Kolek)
   *The Ghost Chronicles: A Medium and a Paranormal Scientist
      Investigate 17 True Hauntings*
   *A Ghost A Day: 365 True Tales of the Spectral, Supernatural,
      And Just Plain Scary!*
   More Ghost Chronicles: Stories from the Realm of the Unknown

Fiction Books by B.T. Lord
   The Twin Ponds Mystery Series
   The Coffin Islands Paranormal Mystery Series

Non-Fiction Books by Bety Comerford (writing with Steve Wilson)
   Ghost and Shamanic Tales of True Hauntings
   The Reluctant Empath
   The Empath's Quest: Finding Your Destiny
   The Empathic Ghost Hunter
   The Empath and the Dark Road: Struggles that Teach the Gift

B.T. Lord

To the real-life Sasha
A kick-ass Cuban who still hasn't
quite accepted her gifts (but I keep
hoping)

J.S. Stephens

To my grandkids Juliette, Addison,
Levi and Kylie
Always shoot for the moon;
Even if you fall, you land among
the stars. You are my heart

PROLOGUE

It was the property no one went to at night.

Not if they wanted to live.

Over a century before, Meadowlark Asylum had been the premier hospital for those rich enough to afford its luxury care of real or imagined ailments. Built outside the western Massachusetts town of Ashboro in 1869, it featured the latest technology of the time in rehabilitating patients in order for them to re-enter society and live a full and happy life.

Those years were long gone.

Starting in the 1920's, when the rich abandoned the area for Europe, Meadowlark turned to filling its hospital rooms with the poor, the insane and those who had nothing clinically wrong. Their sin was eccentricity, or suffering what today would be diagnosed as stress or PTSD, but which wasn't understood at the time. It was better to stuff these society misfits into an asylum than for their families to continue suffering embarrassment by their unconventional behavior.

By the 1970s, Meadowlark had outlived its usefulness. It might have limped along for a few more years. But what happened on the night of October 31, 1975 killed Meadowlark once and for all.

No one knew exactly what happened. The authorities were zealous in covering everything up. And discrediting any locals who swore they saw small fires and heard the sounds of blood curdling screams echoing throughout that long ago Halloween night.

The fact that Meadowlark Asylum was built miles from town, isolated in the middle of dense woods, fueled their assertions that the inhabitants of Ashboro couldn't possibly know what happened. They lived too far away to have witnessed anything.

They put about the story that it was simply a case of the asylum outliving its usefulness.

But the rumors persisted.

The building was shut down and its records burned. In time, the lush forests that surrounded the once beautiful facility and manicured lawns reclaimed the property, leaving it to rot in the shadows of the Berkshire Mountains. The stunning red brick exterior of the hospital was soon buried beneath thick, bulging vines and decades of grime. The ornate wrought iron gates that had once graced the entrance were rusted and hanging off its hinges. The overall appearance was of neglect and dilapidation.

It was then the evil began.

No one knew exactly when Meadowlark began to gain its reputation as one of the most haunted buildings in America. It was said no animals or birds ventured anywhere near the property; bodies of dead crows were frequently found littering the overgrown lawns.

Nor could anyone keep straight which stories about the asylum were true, and which were urban legend. What was clear was that once the sun went down, it was unsafe to stay on the isolated grounds.

Within the abandoned building itself, with its peeling walls, deserted beds and overlooked rooms where supposed horrors took place, there lived a malevolence so dark and malicious that the few who encountered it were never the same; their minds broken by whatever it was they'd seen and experienced.

Was it the spirits of the insane patients? Was it the memory of whatever took place on Halloween night in 1975 seared into time and space? Or, as some darkly claimed, was it the energy left behind by the unspeakable things done to those whose screams were muffled behind the thick walls of the asylum? What was certain was that something vile and inhuman stalked the halls of Meadowlark Asylum, waiting, anticipating, *hungry* for the next victim to walk through its doors.

In the early 2000s, when the subject of ghosts and the paranormal gained popularity on television, a few paranormal investigative teams ventured out to Meadowlark, hoping to capture on film the Monster of the Asylum as the locals called whatever it was that haunted the building. They caught shadows and heard pitiful moaning echoing down the dark hallways. One team caught the unmistakable scratchy sounds of an old 78 record playing. The Monster, however, proved elusive. Yet each team agreed that, although they didn't see the Monster itself, they felt its sinister presence. As if their insides were wrapped in a cold so insidious and consuming, they found it hard to function.

In 2009, a paranormal team from Germany arrived to see if they could get to the bottom of the hauntings. All was going well until a crew member died under mysterious circumstances. It was then the authorities stepped in and put a stop to any further investigations of any kind.

The rumors, however, proved irresistible to the local teenagers. They loved to spray paint the boarded-up windows and doors, and hold loud, raucous parties beneath the beautiful oaks. But once the sun began its descent, they knew to leave. Unless you had a death wish, you didn't stay at Meadowlark Asylum once the sun went down.

Ten years went by in which no one was legally allowed to enter the building. Then, word spread throughout Ashboro that Meadowlark Asylum was once again opening its doors, this time to a world famous paranormal investigative team. Their attempts at finding the Monster of the Asylum would be aired live on TV as a Halloween night special.

The townspeople shook their heads in bewilderment. Didn't these people know they were going into that place on the 44th anniversary of the mysterious incident that closed down the asylum? Weren't they told about the paranormal investigator who had lost his life in a place he never should have been in? Were they unaware of the evil that roamed its decaying corridors?

Was the need for fame so great they were willing to die for it?

While the inhabitants of Ashboro fretted and worried about what was about to happen, within the crumbling walls of Meadowlark Asylum, the Monster rejoiced. It had patiently waited all these years.

It was inevitable. Humans don't like mysteries. They don't respect the unknown. They need to understand everything.

It had known this day would come. The mystery was too great. Too tantalizing not to explore.

It was ready.

I'll be waiting for you. I'll open the door and let you in.

Come inside to die.

If you dare.

CHAPTER ONE

Early May

"This is where, 75 years ago, the remains of two bodies were found. They'd been murdered and stuffed in that niche over there. Since this building became a restaurant in the early 2000s, waitstaff have consistently refused to enter the basement. They swear they hear groans of pain. Stock items keep getting moved around. Their most recent bartender quit when he claimed he came down here one night and was shoved against the wall by unseen hands."

Tina Landry barely heard Devon Watson's words. Her concentration was instead focused on the mass of cobwebs hanging all around her in the dark, dank basement. She had an uncontrollable fear of spiders; when she was a child, her mother found a big black hairy spider burrowed in her ear. Now, surrounded by the hideous things, with their fat black bodies and beady black eyes, it was all she could do not to turn around and run back up the stairs. Her reverie was shattered when she felt a sudden tug on her arm. A moment later she heard Devon's angry whisper in her ear.

"Dammit. Focus, will you? The cameras are rolling." He stepped back and said aloud, "So Tina, are you getting anything?"

With the cameras focused on her, she couldn't tell him to screw himself, as much as she wanted to.

The tall, willowy brunette grudgingly walked over to the niche. She closed her eyes and took in a deep breath.

What's the point of doing this? No matter what I get, he

dismisses it anyway.

Five years ago on a lark, she'd answered an ad in a local newspaper from a paranormal investigative team looking for a psychic to join their ranks. Having grown up with what she called 'knowings' – instances when something she felt was going to happen actually did occur, she thought it would be fun exploring the paranormal. Little did she know how meeting Devon Watson, Mark Parsons and Brandon Middleton would change her life.

At first physically attracted to the tall, handsome Devon, with his longish blond hair and blue eyes, it wasn't long before she realized that behind the good looks lurked an arrogant, egotistical ass who enjoyed giving orders and having them instantly obeyed. Afraid that his partner Mark would be the same, she was pleasantly surprised to discover that the dark haired, dark eyed, slightly shy man was actually a genuinely nice guy. As Devon's right-hand man, he was much too happy being in his friend's shadow. Naturally more reserved than the outgoing Devon, he always gave in to him, even if he didn't agree with the man's decisions or ideas.

Brandon was the jokester in the group. Short, with flaming red hair and the map of Ireland stamped on his face, the only thing he took seriously was the technical equipment he was in charge of.

Although she considered quitting in those moments when Devon became particularly unbearable, Mark and Brandon's calm, funny presence always made her change her mind.

Then the television show happened.

One of their videos showing the unmistakable figure of a man dressed in 18th century clothing standing in the doorway of a colonial-era house went viral on social media. A network executive saw it and quickly offered them a television deal.

Almost from the moment their show debuted, it became a fan favorite and they were now known worldwide as The Ghost Dudes.

To Tina's dismay, Devon's controlling personality and out of control ego grew worse. She found herself becoming increasingly angry at the way he treated her off camera. He belittled her ideas for the show, and thought of her more as the token female than as an equal partner in their team.

Her biggest complaint revolved around his determination to ridicule her abilities. Although she'd joined the group with minimal psychic experience, she found to her surprise that she was beginning to actually connect more with the Other Side during their investigations. She increasingly felt the spirits' emotions – their fear, anger, grief, sorrow. Sometimes she heard their words filtering through her head. Occasionally she even saw a face appear in her mind's eye. Yet no matter how hard she tried to explain that to Devon, he only cared if it led to higher ratings.

His obsessive need for his group to become the top ghost investigative team on television was quickly turning him into someone she barely recognized. Several weeks before, she'd discovered just how far he was willing to go to secure the top spot.

During an investigation of a haunted farmhouse in the countryside of central Pennsylvania, Devon had suddenly feigned a queasy stomach, causing him to leave the set. Suspicious over his uncharacteristic behavior – Devon *never* gave up an opportunity to be on camera - Tina quietly followed him as he hurried down the hallway. Hiding in the shadows, she watched in shock and dismay as he slipped into one of the nearby bedrooms and pushed an antique vase to the edge of an old dresser.

At first not understanding his actions, it soon became clear when, returning to the group, he announced they would next search the very bedroom he'd just come out of. Entering the room, the vibration of their footsteps on the old floorboards caused the vase to crash to the floor.

"Did you see that!" Devon quickly exclaimed to the

camera. "The vase was thrown off the dresser by unseen hands. Maybe whoever threw it doesn't want us in this room."

She'd been appalled at his blatant dishonesty.

Looking back over the two years they'd been on television, she now understood just how many similar stunts he'd pulled. It was what kept their show so popular. They were known as the group who achieved results, and Devon guarded that reputation zealously. He monitored the paranormal blogs and social media, and if someone dared doubt their authenticity, he immediately responded with anger and indignation. A few times he even threatened legal action.

Since that night in Pennsylvania, she grappled with telling the others what she'd seen. But at the end of the day, she kept quiet. The cameramen had to know what was going on. So did Mark and Brandon. She was the only fool who hadn't figured out what Devon was doing. Yet each time she decided to quit, to keep her own integrity intact even as they willingly sold theirs, she held back. Their fame was growing. She was now recognized on the streets. People wanted her autograph. Promotors begged her to appear at various paranormal conventions. Money was pouring in. How could she throw all of that away?

It was a decision that gnawed at her.

As much as she wanted to remain in the limelight, she just couldn't do it by lying to their fans. She'd always prided herself on her trustworthiness. On her ability to clearly tell right from wrong. To ease her guilt, she attempted to talk to Devon. To make him see reason. With her growing abilities, they didn't need gimmicks to keep their TV show going. But their talks always deteriorated into arguments which ended the same way.

"There are lots of pretty girls out there just waiting to take your place."

"I'm more than just a pretty face," she'd yell back. "I'm a valuable member of this team!"

"Yeah, keep telling yourself that."

His insults inevitably left her angry at him and angry at herself. She wasn't sure she had the strength of character to walk away so easily from the fame and glory.

Now she found herself standing in front of the niche trying to concentrate on picking up ghostly activity, while at the same time keeping an eye on the encroaching spiders.

Focus, focus. I need to focus.

In an attempt to shake off her frustration and get this investigation over with so she could get the hell out of this basement and away from these damn spiders, Tina moved out of the light and into the shadows. Turning her head, she gave a quick glance at the camera crew and the red light over the video cameras. This was it. She had to do something. She needed to perform. The camera crew wouldn't wait forever. Nor would Devon, who was glaring at her to get on with it.

Tina closed her eyes to block out her surroundings. Sometimes controlling her breath helped to get her into that quiet place. But there were days when that didn't seem to be enough. Unfortunately, today was one of those days.

With that last thought in mind, she forced herself to take several deep consecutive breaths, releasing them slowly. Anxiety level still high, it took her longer than normal to close out the sounds around her. Finally, after what felt like an eternity, but was only a few moments, she felt it. The prickly sensation starting in the center of her forehead. The hairs on her arms stood at attention as the air around her swayed. Shifted.

Tina whispered, "I am picking something up. Someone is here."

"Do they want to talk with us?" Both Devon and Mark asked in unison.

Tina reach out with her mind. "Do you wish to communicate with us? Can you tell us who you are?" she asked the energy swirling around her.

The tingling around her shoulders increased as a chill ran down her spine. A spirit was present, standing very close to her. A masculine energy enveloped her, indicating the spirit was a male. She caught her breath as a sudden sharp pain hit her in the back of her head. Unable at first to recognize what she was feeling, the pain grew stronger. More insistent. Coming at her in waves. Accompanying the pain was a fear and agitation so overwhelming, her limbs began to shake.

A sickening, squishing sound filled her ears. It sounded suspiciously like a hammer smashing into a melon.

Tina gasped aloud when she suddenly recognized what she was experiencing.

Oh my God, the spirit was bludgeoned to death! He knew he was going to die, and there was nothing he could do to save himself. I'm feeling his last terrifying moments on earth.

For the first time in her life, she smelled the foul odor of sweat. Sensed his terror over his impending death. Felt the agony as he was bludgeoned over and over again. Overwhelmed by the unexpected sensation, she visibly jerked. And abruptly lost the connection. As quickly as she'd felt the presence, it was gone.

"What the hell was that? Are you okay, Tina?" Mark asked in concern.

What could she say? That her own fear had caused her to break the link?

"Tell us who you see," Devon said, playing to the camera. In a whisper, he snarled, "Pretend like you're getting something, will you?" The harshness of his words stung. "These camera guys aren't going to stick around forever."

Tina struggled to reach out again, to try and call on the spirit to once again connect with her. Yet the EMF meter Devon held in his hand remained frustratingly silent.

The pressure mounted as she felt everyone's eyes on her. Should she be honest and say she'd lost the connection? Should she risk Devon's annoyance and disgust by telling the truth?

The decision was taken out of her hands when, to her surprise, the meter suddenly began beeping, its red lights blinking furiously.

"Wow, there we go. We have a presence here with us," Devon cried out.

Upset at her inability to regain the connection with the spirit, she glanced down at the glowing lights on the meter which Devon held close to her hip. Her distress quickly turned to anger.

"What does the spirit look like, Tina? Tell us," Devon urged in a voice that she knew all too well. Glancing over at the cameramen, she saw the eagerness on their faces. Even Mark looked pleased. The Ghost Dudes had done it again. They'd captured proof of the existence of ghosts.

Tina wanted nothing more than to shout at Devon to shove it and stomp out of there. She was sick and tired of his bullshit. But even as she opened her mouth to protest, she swallowed her words. It was no use. She'd signed a contract. She needed to go through with this charade.

Even if it tore her up inside.

Weaving in what they'd been told of the murders with what she'd physically felt, Tina described her experience. As she spoke, the meter continued to go off, sending her further into depression. When she was done, she found herself drained and exhausted.

"Great. Cut. We got what we need," one of the cameramen finally said. "It's a wrap."

Tina waited until Mark and the cameramen went upstairs before she grabbed Devon and pulled him aside. "You gave me your phone to hold. You did that on purpose, didn't you? You saw me put it in my pocket and you knew if you held the meter up next to it, the device would go off."

"So what? You weren't doing anything. I had to save the show. As usual." Seeing how upset she was, he reached out to grasp her by the forearm. "Come on. Let's go. We still have the reveal to get through."

Incensed at his inability to understand that what he was doing was wrong, Tina swatted him away. "Keep your hands off me. Your ego is going to destroy us one of these days."

"Look who's talking. You're a bigger fake than I am." He pitched his voice high in a pathetic attempt to imitate her. "Oooooh, I sense the presence of a spirit." He rolled his eyes. "Yeah, right."

"That's not true. I told you I've been getting more stuff." She quickly described what she'd felt just a few short moments before.

"Then why didn't you hold on to the connection? Why did your body jerk the way it did?"

She stammered. "Because it was so strong – I'd never felt anything like that before."

Devon rolled his eyes. "For Chrissakes, Tina, that's your job. You're the psychic, remember? You're *supposed* to make a connection and hold onto it." He sighed angrily. "Jeez, you can't even do that right." Before she could defend herself, he abruptly stuck his finger in her face. "Listen, I don't care if you actually connect or not. I don't give a rat's ass if you actually feel someone dying. Bottom line is that, in front of the camera, you make it *look* like you're doing your job. Make it up if you have to. But do not screw this gig up. We're going to be the biggest thing ever in the paranormal community. So either get onboard, or get out."

"You're an ass, Devon Watson."

He brought his face close to hers. "Yeah, but I'll be a rich ass."

He turned abruptly and went up the stairs, leaving Tina alone.

Shaking over the encounter, she struggled yet again with the idea of quitting. Was it worth compromising her integrity for a television show? Was it worth getting constantly insulted by that dipshit? Damn it, her abilities *were* growing, despite what Devon believed. Maybe it was time to walk away with her honor and honesty intact.

"Tina, get up here, they're ready for you now. It's your turn to be interviewed," Mark yelled down the stairs.

Shit.

"Come on, you're holding things up!"

Pushing aside her last thought, and heaving a loud, discouraging sigh, she grudgingly went up the stairs.

***

"You can't be serious," Tina said.

"As serious as a heart attack," Devon laughed out loud.

It was a week after the investigation. After calling an emergency meeting of his team, she, Mark, and Brandon were now seated in Devon's kitchen.

"So here's the deal. The ratings just came in and we're slipping. Ghost investigation shows are popping up all over TV. We're no longer unique. I've been talking to the network execs and we all agree we need something spectacular to recapture the public's attention. If not, we're toast at the end of the year."

"How exactly are we supposed to do that?" Mark asked.

Devon handed each of them a flyer. "Feast your eyes on this."

DO YOU HAVE WHAT IT TAKES TO INVESTIGATE A HAUNTED LOCATION? ARE YOU READY TO TEAM UP WITH THE WORLD-FAMOUS GHOST DUDES AS THEY EXPLORE ONE OF AMERICA'S MOST HAUNTED BUILDINGS?

Tina read the flyer and stared at him in disbelief.

"Think about it," Devon continued. "What better way to get us back on top than to offer a team the chance to shadow us on an investigation? A majority of ghost groups were started because of our show. Now one of those teams gets the honor of working with us. We'll broadcast live to allow viewers at home to investigate right along with us. We'll make it interactive so they can communicate with Brandon via text and let us know if they see anything."

Brandon threw the flyer back onto the table. "This is about as foolproof as the Titanic. We have no guarantees we won't end up with a seasoned team who will outshine and outmaneuver us. Or stumble onto things they have no business stumbling onto." He gave Devon a knowing look.

"Save it," Tina spoke up. "I know all about your dishonest shenanigans."

Devon turned to her. "My so called dishonest shenanigans is what put your face on the cover of People Magazine." He turned his attention back to Brandon. "No worries, my friend. I've got it covered. We get final approval on who the team will be that wins our contest. We'll just make sure to pick a team of young, starstruck teenagers who can be easily manipulated."

Tina's jaw dropped. "You're seriously suggesting we manipulate a group of kids?"

"Sure. Why not?"

She groaned. "Investigations are not a joke, Devon. Someone could get hurt. Sometimes I think you've lost your mind."

"They'll be fine," Devon said as he slapped his copy of the flyer on the table between them. "We'll make sure they're with at least one of us at all times. And should they trip and hurt themselves, the network is having their families sign a liability waiver. It's a win/win situation. They get to go out with their heroes, and we get a ratings bonanza."

"If we agree to do this, do we have a location yet?" Mark

asked.

"Since I knew you guys would be onboard, I already gave the okay. They're scouting locations now."

As always, it took a moment for Mark to respond. When he did, Tina felt her stomach clench in disgust. "Whatever, dude. If you think this will work, I'm on board."

Of course you are, you spineless fool.

Devon leaned forward and he and Mark did a palm slap. "Way to be a team player."

Brandon shrugged. "Count me in as well."

Devon looked to Tina for her response. Instead of automatically agreeing like the others, she remained silent, her arms tightly crossed against her chest. Her posture and facial expression spoke volumes. He knew she was upset he'd made such a monumental decision without discussing it with the team first. But hey, too bad. This was *his* team. He'd brought them together. He'd busted his ass doing everything possible to keep them on top. Hell, he'd even come up with their name. Because of that, he had every right to make any and all decisions that impacted the future of his team.

Devon felt confident she'd get with the program. If not, he had no problem filling her shoes with someone who wasn't so obnoxious to him. Seriously, with everything he was doing to keep them on the air, you think she'd be a little more appreciative.

Ignoring Tina, he spoke directly to Mark, "Although we don't have a location yet, we do know when we're going to air the show." He looked at each of them, excitement on his face. "What better time to investigate America's most haunted location than on the spookiest night of the year? That's right. We're doing our live broadcast on Halloween night." He gleefully rubbed his hands together. "We're gonna rock our fans' world. They won't know what hit them. The Ghost Dudes will rule again!"

***

Sixteen year old Sasha Marquez elbowed her way into the small circle. "Did you guys see this?" She unrolled the newspaper, flipping it open to the Talk of the Town section. "It's too unbelievable." She tapped her neon colored fingernails on the half page ad. "The Ghost Dudes are running a contest. They're looking for a paranormal group to investigate right alongside them!"

Levi Taylor jumped off his seat and snatched the newspaper for a closer look, "No way. That is beyond cool."

"Exactly. You know what this means, don't you? If we win the contest, we'll be famous. We might even get our own TV show."

Sasha's mind reeled with the possibilities. The 5 ft. 3-inch Latina had always dreamed of making it big. Of finding a way to escape this small, suffocating western Massachusetts town. She could see it now. Sasha Marquez, famous photographer with the uncanny ability to capture proof of the paranormal. A feat that many had attempted, but none had mastered. Even though she hadn't actually captured anything even remotely resembling anything paranormal, how hard could it be? She had tons of experience taking pictures as the high school paper's resident photographer. And hadn't her photography instructor declared she was a natural? With an excellent, creative eye?

"Earth to Sasha," Addison Monroe laughed as she waved her hand back and forth in front of Sasha's face. "Your name isn't up in lights yet." She and Levi chuckled. "I agree, it sounds like fun. But did you read the fine print below the contest rules? It specifically states that a five-minute video needs to be submitted, explaining why we believe our team should be selected to win." She flipped her blonde hair behind her ears. "Not to sound like a buzz kill, but we don't have a team."

"Sure we do," Sasha said as she pointed to each of them. "Presto. Instant team."

Addison rolled her eyes. "Let's be real. Although we've watched The Ghost Dudes and we know what goes into an investigation, we've never actually done one of our own. How are we going to pull it off? There's only three of us. We have no equipment, and no money to buy what we need."

"I'm sure if we put our heads together, we can figure something out," Sasha replied. "I have some babysitting money stashed away."

"I thought that was your Escape Millbrook Fund," Levi said.

"Well, duh. Getting on The Ghost Dudes and becoming famous will get us out of Millbrook a lot faster than me babysitting that little horror Brittany Holmes. Think about it. As soon as our faces show up on TV, we'll probably get dozens of offers from Hollywood agents. I'd say that's worth dipping into my escape fund."

"I don't know." He looked to Addison to gauge her response. "The obvious has already been pointed out. We have no money. And there's only three of us. The Ghost Dudes have four members on their team, each with a specific role. Obviously, Sash, you'd be the photographer, but what about Addison and I? Even if we could afford equipment, who would we get to man basecamp?"

"Come on, you guys. Have a little faith," Sasha pleaded. "This could be our one chance to do something to change our destiny. Instead of just watching The Ghost Dudes, we could *be* the next Ghost Dudes." Her grin widened. "We're younger. We're smarter. And we're a lot better looking." Both Addison and Levi gave her a dubious look. With her short spiky hair, now dyed orange this week to fit her whim, her penchant for wearing black, and her ears studded with over a dozen earrings, she wasn't exactly the poster child for sophisticated fashion.

Nervous that they weren't onboard yet, she added, "Levi, you could do what Mark Parsons does on the show. You'd make a perfect EVP specialist. Don't you still have that digital recorder your dad bought you to help study for the history finals?" Levi nodded. "Awesome! It's not rocket science to hold a recorder and ask, 'is there someone here with us' a bazillion times." She spun towards Addison. "You can be the team psychic, like Tina Landry."

Addison gasped. "Say what?"

"You know the role of the psychic would be great for you." She placed her hand on Addison's shoulder. "Listen, I know your Mom is all freaked out about your Aunt Juliette being a little different. Okay. A lot different. Okay, really, really different. But you are more like her than you want to admit." She softened her voice and gave Addison a reassuring smile, "Don't you remember last fall when half the class was scouring the softball fields for Mr. Holland's wedding ring? The one he lost when pitching the last inning?" Addison remained silent and Sasha hurriedly continued. "Think about it, Addy. More than fifteen students searched those fields for over 3 hours. Yet, the next day, when I told you what happened, you had me drive you to the field. You stepped out of my car, closed your eyes, walked a couple of feet and picked up the gold band! It was like unbelievable!" She shook her head to herself. "I still can't figure out how you did it."

Addison nervously shifted her stance. "Yeah, and when I returned it to good ol' Mr. Holland, he all but accused me of staging the whole thing in order to get all the attention. It took my History teacher to remind him I wasn't even in Millbrook when he lost the ring in the first place."

"Some people just can't admit when they're wrong," Sasha replied blithely. "Anyway, I think I've made my point. Addison, you'll be our psychic."

"I don't like attention, you know that. And I especially don't like the idea of going on TV and pretending to be a psychic. It's too much pressure."

Sasha looked at her friend. What Addison was saying was true. Although she was pretty and sweet and could have any boy in high school, she was also modest and very reserved. She loathed being the center of anything.

Sasha had to think fast if she had any hope of salvaging the situation.

"Do you remember the essay we had to write a few weeks ago in English class? The one that asked us how we'd like to change the world if we could?" Addison nodded. "Do you remember what you wrote?"

"Yeah. I said I'd like to find a way to bring people together. To stop all the arguing and hatred and fear. To help us feel good about ourselves so we didn't need to put others down in order to make ourselves feel better."

"That's right." Sasha slid into the stone seat next to her. "So why can't you do that on TV?"

Addison looked at her warily. "And how would I do that?"

"Look, it's obvious you have a gift. Not only did you find Mr. Holland's ring like that" – she snapped her fingers – "but I remember you warning me not to drive down Hickory Road last summer. I didn't know what you were talking about, but I'm glad I listened because a huge tree fell down across the road right around the time I would have been driving there. Maybe I would have been hit, maybe it would have missed me. But the point is, you knew something was going to happen on Hickory Road and it did."

"I still don't get where you're going with this."

Sasha sighed. "You're a bazillion times better than Tina Landry. You go on The Ghost Dudes, you show them what you can do and you make other kids who are watching know they're not freaks. You'd be an example to millions of teenagers who may be struggling, like you, to come to terms that they have a gift."

Addison stared at her. "That's the biggest crock I've ever heard," she exclaimed.

"But it's true and you know it."

Addison nervously bit her lip and Sasha inwardly rejoiced. Whenever she bit her lip, the Latina knew she'd won her over.

Levi spoke up. "Now what? We still don't have computer equipment for a basecamp, or the means to make a video. And we still need a technology expert."

Surprised that she was actually warming up to what Sasha had told her, Addison interjected. "What about that new kid who's been trying to start a technology club?"

"That dweeb?" Levi gasped. "You mean, what's his name, Sam...Stu..."

"Stan..." Addison snapped her fingers, "Crane. That's his name. Stan Crane."

Sasha elbowed Levi. "I told you she was psychic."

"No, you dope," Addison retorted. "I sit behind him in social studies."

Levi groaned. "He tried to start up a technology group last January. He had a total of one attendee. And that's only because the kid was trying to get out of detention. I actually kinda felt sorry for him. There he was in the cafeteria, surrounded by all these computers he'd dragged in and he was the only member of his tech club." He shook his head sadly. "It was pathetic."

"Do you have a better idea?" Sasha retorted. "He's the only one we know who really understands computers."

"You guys can't be serious," Levi continued. "Have you ever heard him talk? He sounds like a friggin' computer. He has no friends. He dresses like a complete nerd. He creeps me out."

"He creeps you out because he's intelligent and all you're interested in is fast cars, pretty girls, and trying to outdo yourself in crazy ass stunts. I say we at least talk to him."

"You're not going to understand anything he says."

"We'll take our chances."

Levi sighed. "I'm telling you, if you bring that geek into this, you're going to regret it."

CHAPTER TWO

Stan Crane pulled his hand through his shaggy light brown hair and sighed in frustration.

Another crappy day in the neighborhood.

Another day of dodging insults at school from moronic jocks who could barely spell their names. Another afternoon spilling his books on the school bus because Brian Nesbro stuck his foot out and tripped him as he walked down the aisle, sending the entire bus into peals of harsh laughter.

God, he hated this town and everyone in it.

He and his parents had relocated to Millbrook from Boston last August after his dad accepted a lucrative job as a technical engineering manager at a nearby software company.

From the first, Stan found it hard to adjust to life in what he considered the sticks. Accustomed to the hustle and bustle of the city, Millbrook was as exciting as watching the grass grow. It didn't help that he instantly became pegged as the high school nerd. Just because he loved computers, he was treated as if he had two heads. Hadn't these people ever heard of Steve Jobs? Bill Gates? Friggin' Microsoft? They'd never be able to get through their days without their iPhones, iPads, their social media accounts. Without computers, they'd be nowhere.

What was it going to take to get people to quit ridiculing him, making him feel less worthy than they were because he wore glasses and used big words when he spoke? It wasn't as if he didn't try to fit in. It wasn't his fault he sucked at sports. Or preferred tinkering on the antique computers that filled his family garage instead of joining the athletes in trying to figure out whose bicep was bigger. At least the old boxy PCs didn't care if his clothes weren't perfectly coordinated, or if his black rimmed glasses kept falling down his nose. They never laughed when his nerves caused him to stutter sometimes, or if he blushed at inconvenient moments. Still, as much as he tried to ignore the pain in his gut whenever the kids at school gave him that 'it's the loser' look, it hurt. A lot.

The sad part was that Stan had no idea how to be cool.

To know the right thing to say at the right time. To say anything at all that didn't sound completely nerdy or nonsensical to the technologically illiterate. To not want to melt into the floor whenever he saw Addison Monroe at school.

He smiled at the image of her curly blonde hair, green eyes and beautiful smile. She was one of the few classmates who didn't treat him as if he had fleas.

But who was he kidding? A pretty girl like that would never give him the time of day. She was way out of his league.

His only chance of impressing her was to show he was more than a computer geek. He needed to do something outstanding that she couldn't ignore. Something that would make him stand out.

"What do you think?" he asked Mr. Winston, his mother's fluffy grey and white Norwegian Forest cat that sat on one of the shelves in the garage, silently watching him. "The theory of relativity's already been invented. I can start working on a time machine, but who knows how much *time* that's going to take. Haha. Maybe I can become a Marvel Comics superhero. That would impress the shit out of her, for sure. I can become Captain Fantastic who vaporizes assholes with a single stare. Oh wait. That would destroy half this town."

Mr. Winston blinked his large yellow eyes. "Yeah, you're right. I gotta think bigger than that. It's going to take someone real special to win Addison's heart."

He quickly shut up when the door that separated the garage

from the house opened and his mother appeared. She looked at the dozens of computers and shook her head in disgust.

"I thought I told you to organize this stuff. There's so much garbage in here, it's going to take you forever to put it all away. Before you know it, winter will be here, and I have no intention of digging my car out from under a blanket of snow when I have a perfectly good garage I can park in."

Stan mentally rolled his eyes. How his mother loved to exaggerate! She could see a spider crawling across the kitchen floor and make it sound as though they were about to be invaded by a horde of gi-normous tarantulas.

When she got into one of these moods, it was better to humor her.

"First of all, Mom, this isn't garbage. These are historical antiques from our not too distant technological past. Second of all, I'm working on it. It's just going to take some time. Dad wants all similar parts stacked together and –"

"I don't care what your father wants. I'm telling you I want this stuff either put on those shelves or gotten rid of. I'm not running a home for lost computer parts."

She slammed the door behind her.

"I don't think Mom realized she actually made a funny statement," Stan said to Mr. Winston.

Mr. Winston yawned.

Stan gazed lovingly at the sight of so many old, discarded computers and their resident parts. What could he say? His adoration for computers ran in the family. Dad lived and breathed technology, and was forever collecting antiquated PCs and the like and stashing them in the garage. He could open his own museum of obsolete computers if he wanted.

Hey, maybe that was Stan's way of getting out of Millbrook. He could charge people money to walk through their garage and peer at computers that dated back to the 1990s. Wouldn't that just make a wonderful entry in their diary? What I did on my summer vacation.

Yeah, right.

"No point in procrastinating any further," he said as he stood up. "Gotta get my posterior in gear and start moving this stuff onto the shelves, or Mom will make my life a living hell."

He turned and was about to hoist one of the computers up into his arms when he heard the ear splitting sounds of death metal echoing up the quiet suburban street. It was May, and with the temperatures starting to warm up, he'd kept the garage door open to try and get some air.

Turning his long, lanky body, he watched in astonishment as a ratty old, purple Honda Civic that looked as though it was being held together with rubber bands pulled up to the curb outside his driveway. A moment later, the radio went off, returning the neighborhood to blessed silence. Wondering who the hell could be parking in the front of his house, and in such a piece of shit car, he was shocked when Sasha Marquez climbed out of the driver's side. When the passenger side door opened, he almost fainted.

Shit! It's Addison Monroe!

A moment later, the two ladies were joined by Levi Taylor exiting the back seat.

He knew the three were friends. Whenever he saw them around school, they were always together. They showed up together, had pretty much the same classes together, ate together and went home together. If he didn't know better, he'd swear they were tied together with some kind of invisible rope. What often puzzled him was why they were friends in the first place. You couldn't find three people so different from each other.

Levi was tall, built like an athlete and good looking, with dark hair, hazel eyes, a devilish smile and an air of invincibility. His father was a transplanted cop from New York City who now worked as the Chief of Police for the Millbrook Police Department. If there was anyone who should feel like a fish out of water, it would be Levi, with his strong New York City accent and citified ways. But he appeared to be the type of guy who took nothing seriously. He treated the world as a place that needed to be challenged on a daily basis. Stan heard stories about his love of speed and daredevil escapades. It was said he'd borrowed a friend's jeep and drove down what was known as Suicide Drop – a steep cliff wall that opened out to the Hockamac River that skirted Millbrook. How he'd done that without breaking his neck was anyone's guess. But somehow Levi had lived to tell the tale.

A part of him believed Levi insane to take so many chances. He'd be lucky if he saw his thirtieth birthday. The other part, however, admired Levi's courage and his casual attitude to everything. He had balls of steel as far as Stan was concerned, while his were probably made up of circuit boards and colored wires.

Although he'd never own up to it, the diminutive Sasha Marquez intimidated the crap out of him. Always dressed in goth-like black, with spiky hair that, at least this week was orange, she wore a gazillion earrings in her earlobes and exuded an air of 'don't you even think of messing with me'. He knew she lived with her widowed mother in what was considered the poorer side of town. Being one of the few, if not the only Cuban American family in Millbrook, she had a chip on her shoulder that wasn't hard to miss.

Why pretty, sweet, quiet Addison hung around with these two was beyond him.

"Yo, Stan," Sasha called out. "We need to talk." The three friends walked into the garage. Planting her black boots on the floor, she put her hands on her hips and looked around. "Now this is what I'm talking about." She glanced at Levi. "Voila. Instant equipment for basecamp."

"I'm still not convinced," Levi replied.

"That's because you didn't think of this yourself." She walked over to a pile of computers and started browsing. "This stuff work?"

"No," Stan answered, puzzled by their presence in his garage.

"Can you get them up and running? Like last week?"

"Only if you tell me what this is all about."

Sasha strode up to him and shoved a piece of paper in his face. "That's why, Computer Man." Stan took the paper and read it. When he was done, he jerked his head up in surprise. Sasha grinned. "That's right, bro. We're going to be famous."

"Do you know how popular The Ghost Dudes are?" he stammered, stunned at what they were proposing. "You're going to be competing with hundreds, if not thousands of other paranormal investigative teams who actually are teams and actually have experience investigating ghosts."

"What's so hard about finding ghosts?" she asked dismissively.

"It's more than just waving a spectral carrot and asking them to come out of hiding, you know."

She lifted a black eyebrow. "What do you know about investigating ghosts? You ever see a ghost? You ever talk to a ghost? You ever take a picture of a ghost?"

"Have you?"

She grinned. "I will once I'm on TV."

Stan grew flustered as he felt the hot blush on his face. His embarrassment grew when, as usually happened when he was nervous, he began to stutter. "Listen, I – I read a lot, and this isn't stuff you—you should take lightly."

"Oh, so you think when we win this contest, we're going to get eaten by demons or something?"

Levi barked out a laugh.

"What Sasha is trying to say," Addison interjected, "and not very well, is that in order for our team to be complete, we need a computer technician. We couldn't think of anyone who knows computers better than you. Are you game? Do you want to join us?"

To their surprise, he took a step back and glared at them. "I--I don't appreciate being jerked around," he snapped.

"We're not, honestly. We need someone who can set up the video and audio equipment and man basecamp. You've seen The Ghost Dudes on TV. You know how important the tech guy is. We need someone who's responsible, and who we can trust to watch our backs." Addison pointed to Levi and Sasha. "Levi is going to be our EVP expert. Sasha already takes pictures for the high school newspaper so she's our photographer."

"And what are you going to do?" Stan asked.

She looked uncomfortable as she muttered in a low voice, "I'm the psychic."

His eyes widened, but he caught himself from chortling out loud and embarrassing her further.

"You…um…you have—er—gifts?"

"Bro, you don't know the half of what this girl can do," Sasha spoke up.

Although Levi had been against bringing Stan onto the team, the sight of all the computers quickly changed his mind. There had to be thousands of dollars' worth of equipment just sitting in this garage. It was more than enough to suit their needs.

"Listen Stan, we're in a bind here. We can't afford to buy all the stuff we need. If you can get just a couple of these computers up and running, you're in," Levi explained. "That is, if you want to become a member of The Ghost Seekers."

"Cool name, huh?" Sasha grinned. "We came up with it last night."

Stan looked into each of their faces and saw how serious they were about all of this. He could only guess at their motives since, as far as he knew, they'd never shown any interest before in anything even remotely paranormal. If he were smart, he'd refuse. He knew absolutely nothing about ghosts, but had read enough horror novels and watched enough scary movies to know they weren't something you messed with.

And he still wasn't sure they weren't luring him in just to pull the rug out from under him and laugh at his pathetic attempt to be their friend.

Yet, he had to admit, he was intrigued. He didn't think they had a chance of winning the contest. They had zero experience and would probably pee themselves if they actually saw a ghost.

But what if we do win? What if we really get a chance to be on TV with The Ghost Dudes? I'll be the famous computer technician who watches my team's back and warns them when they're in danger. I might even be the one who saves their butts from a scary apparition.

I'll finally be somebody in this one-horse town. How can I not do this?

"I'll join under one condition."

"And that is?" Addison asked.

"That you don't call me Stan."

Sasha frowned. "Dude, that's your name."

He shook his head. "Since we're starting this new venture, I don't want to be known as Stan, the computer nerd anymore."

"So what do you want to be called?" Sasha questioned. "Portal Boy? Alexa Man? Apple Watch Wally?"

He raised his gaze until he met hers. With his heart pounding in his chest, he said, "I want to be known as Razor, the man with the sharp intelligence."

Sasha stared back at him before suddenly breaking into giggles.

Levi rolled his eyes. "Seriously, dude?"

Stan prayed the floor would open up and swallow him. Now he felt like a complete idiot for even saying such a thing. How could he be so stupid to trust that they might actually want him, not only on their team, but as a friend?

Addison abruptly felt her stomach clench. At first worrying that she'd eaten something that didn't agree with her, she looked at Stan and it suddenly became crystal clear.

This is so weird, but I think I'm feeling his emotions!

How or why this was happening remained a mystery. But before she could stop it, she felt herself enveloped in his deep sense of loneliness, his yearning to belong. It broke her heart to feel his despair and embarrassment at Sasha's laughter.

He just wants a friend, but he doesn't think he's good enough for us.

Addison came up to him and gently rested her hand on his arm. To her surprise, she felt a strange tingle in her fingers. She saw by the look on his face that he'd felt it too.

"I don't see why not," she whispered. "If that's what you want."

They looked at each other for a long moment before he gave a sharp nod. "I do," he whispered back.

"We need to make a video telling The Ghost Dudes why they should pick us, besides the obvious," Sasha said as she used both hands to point at herself. Oblivious to the odd interplay between Addison and Stan, she added, "You got a video camera?"

Stan forced himself to look away from Addison and focus on Sasha. "There's one on the shelf over there. It's my dad's old model, but it still works."

"Great. If you can think of something snazzy to write up tonight, do it. We'll meet tomorrow at noon at the gazebo in Radley Park and go over what we've got. The sooner we make the video and send it in, the sooner we can get on TV." She looked at each of them and grinned from ear to ear. "Well my friends, I think we have ourselves a paranormal investigative team!" The three slapped palms and turned to Stan who hesitated for a moment before joining in the palm slapping.

"Smart move, Stan the Man!" Sasha called out over her shoulder as she walked towards her car. "You've just made the best decision of your friggin' life! See you *mañana!*"

The three piled back into Sasha's car. A moment later, the air was filled with the mind numbing sounds of death metal as they pulled away from the curb and drove away.

"It's Razor," Stan whispered under his breath after they were gone. "The name is Razor."

CHAPTER THREE

Late May

Thunder roared.

Lightning cracked.

Fingertips pressed against cold glass panes, Addison stared out into the darkness. She glanced up and out of the oversized window, her view briefly illuminated by the flashes of light streaking across the sky. What lay before her appeared to be barren. Nothing more than a field overflowing with bramble bushes. Towering evergreens and long dead oaks lined the edge of the property. This was one of the densest, darkest forests she'd ever seen. A shiver ran up her spine. Her heart pounded in her chest.

Where in God's name was she?

Fingers trembling uncontrollably against the glass, she tried to recall the last thing she remembered.

Think. Think. Hadn't she been with her friends?

Weren't they just hanging out in her bedroom, watching the video of themselves they were going to submit to the Ghost Dudes contest?

If so, where were they now? How the hell had she gotten here? And where exactly was here anyway?

Realizing that if her friends were close by, she wasn't going to find them glued to this window, she forced herself to do something. Anything.

Feeling better for finally making a decision, and in an

attempt to calm her escalating nerves, she inhaled deeply. Not knowing what she'd find, it was all she could do to muster her strength and step away from the window. Doing an about face, she peered into the darkness.

It felt like forever, but her eyes finally adjusted to the dimness surrounding her. She'd always been good at seeing in the dark. At least that's what her Mom told her. Thinking of her mother, and the safety of her arms, brought a sudden tightness to her chest. A longing she hadn't felt since she was very young. Tears welled up in her eyes. She didn't know where she was and she was scared. But she had to figure out what was going on. What choice did she have? Cowering in the corner and waiting for God knows what to happen was not an option.

Gathering her strength once again, she peered around. She appeared to be in some sort of bedroom. It smelled old and musty, with a metal bed frame sitting in the far corner. Her fear increased when she saw the paint flaked walls filled with holes and pieces of plaster littering the floor. Throat dry, voice raspy, she whispered. "Sasha?"

Nothing but silence.

Addison swallowed past the sudden lump in her throat and spoke again. "Levi?"

Something was wrong.

Deathly wrong.

Surely her friends would respond if they could hear her. They would never be so cruel.

Fists clenched, shoulders tense, nerves as tight as piano strings, she raised her voice and tried once more. "Sasha? Levi? Where are you?"

She visibly jumped when she suddenly heard music playing.

A chill ran up her spine when she recognized it. It was one of her mother's favorite songs.

Stairway to Heaven by Led Zeppelin.

Where was it coming from?

Recalling what her aunt had once told her about heightening her senses, Addison closed her eyes. Barely able to hear the tune above the rushing of blood in her ears, she forced herself to calm down. To slow her breathing.

The opening notes of the haunting guitar melody seemed to originate from somewhere in front of her.

What the heck?

Were Sasha and Levi playing a prank on her?

Just the thought that they could be so mean lessened the vice-like grip on her chest. She found herself thinking of what she'd say to them when she did find them.

Anger strengthening her resolve, she found her voice.

"Levi, Sasha. Stop it. I'm serious! Where are you guys?"

Addison jumped again when the loud rumblings of thunder crashed overhead. The floor beneath her feet shook. The room filled with a blue hue, highlighting a doorway at the end of the room. Hurrying towards it, she ducked outside and found herself standing in a long corridor that seemed to stretch on forever. Her footsteps echoed loudly in her ears as she gingerly walked down the hallway. Turning to her right, then to her left, she saw a series of doors lining the corridor. She thought to open one but just as she reached out to grab the doorknob, she hesitated. She had no idea what or who was behind the door. It seemed safer to just keep walking. Eventually she had to come to some sort of exit.

She turned her attention back to the corridor and gasped aloud. In front of her stood a pair of French doors. How was that possible? A moment ago, the hallway had stretched out into the darkness. But now she was facing these doors. Where had they come from?

What was happening to her?

Another loud boom erupted overhead. As if the sky itself had torn itself wide open, angry rain pelted against the roof. She looked back over her shoulder and cried out, "Come on, guys Stop kidding around. This isn't funny!"

Forcing herself forward in an effort to figure out just what game was being played, she grabbed the door handles and flung the doors open. She stepped inside and suddenly found herself standing in a large rectangular room bathed in sunlight. The brightness showed off the rot and decay. Dust covered everything and, much like the other room she'd been in, this too was falling apart and obviously abandoned.

Addison looked to her right. Through the windows, she saw a night as black as death, punctuated with bursts of blue light as the rain threw itself against the glass. Yet how could this be?

Was she mistaken? How someone turned on a bright light?

If they did, where were they? Was it Sasha and Levi? Were they trying to show her where they were?

The thought that either Sasha or Levi were in this room but somehow unable to speak, tore at her. She hated feeling so helpless. Were they in trouble? Damn it, where were they?

A sudden thought slipped in through her fear. Was all this some sort of a macabre master plan - a test to see if she had what it took to be a member of the Ghost Seekers? Could they be so heartless? The sheer thought of it formed a knot in her stomach. Her heart pounded as she muttered, "If I find out that you guys are playing a prank on me, you are so going to be sorry."

Walking further into the room, she began to hear murmurs. Soon the murmurs turned to moans of pain.

"Help us."

Addison's blood ran cold.

No. No. No. This can't be happening. It isn't real.

Quickening her pace, she headed towards the center of the room. The music that had been playing softly in the background suddenly stopped. Whirling about, she brought her hand up to her mouth.

The decay had disappeared. The room had come alive. As

Addison took in the remarkable sight, she saw the area was now brightly lit, with rows of tables and chairs placed in neat rows. From the doors she watched as dozens of men and women shuffled inside. Dressed in tattered and dirty medical gowns, they quietly made their way towards the seats where they sat down. Addison heard the scrape of wood on tile seconds before she caught movement out of the corner of her eye. Turning to find the source, she looked on in horror as an elderly man appeared where moments before there had been only broken plaster and grime. Emaciated, with wisps of gray hair standing on end, his hands were bound to the arms of an oversized wooden chair. He forcibly rocked back and forth, the chair groaning and creaking in response.

Suddenly, a nurse darted out from the shadows and ran straight through her. Addison's body suddenly jerked as a bone cold chill tore through her, almost sending her to her knees. She couldn't believe the nurse had actually walked through her. As if she wasn't there.

The nurse, unaware and apparently unaffected by Addison, stood in front of the patient. She towered over the man still rocking wildly in the chair.

"Samuel, this sort of behavior will not be tolerated! Gerald, take him away. If he refuses his medicine when you get him to his room, you know what to do."

Addison watched helplessly as a tall, burly orderly with dark hair and large piercing blue eyes also came out of the shadows. Striding towards the hapless patient, who cowered at the sight of him, he ripped the restraints from Samuel's wrists, jerked him to his feet and physically dragged him from the room.

What was going on? Why was she here? Why was she seeing all of this?

Frantically looking for a way out, she saw the room bustling with activity. A flurry of people dressed in white uniforms moved past her, pushing metal carts that held medicine in little white cup towards the patients seated at the tables and in the chairs. It took her a moment to realize they too were unaware of her presence.

From the middle of the crowd, a loud male voice rang out above the chaos. "If you know what's good for you, you will do as you're told. You heard Nurse Alice. If you refuse to cooperate, I have permission to do as I see fit."

Addison turned to see that Gerald had returned. He exuded an air of sinister malevolence as he clamped his hands down on either side of a chair in which a frightened, skeletal-like woman sat.

"Don't. Please. I don't want to die. I don't belong here. I told you," she shrieked. "I don't belong here. Why won't you people listen to me?"

Clamoring sounds filled the room as faceless men and woman abruptly bolted from their chairs. Cautiously approaching Gerald and the woman, they began to chant while pumping the air with their fists.

"Fight, fight, fight!"

The chair rocked beneath the old woman as she flung her weight in a continued attempt to dissuade Gerald from hurting her. He stood over her, taking sadistic pleasure in his intimidation of the frail woman.

Addison was filled with rage. How could she just stand here and do nothing? She had to help the woman.

Bounding over to the orderly, she screamed, "What are you doing to her? Leave that poor woman alone, you animal!"

Gerald stood up and slowly turned around. Eyes blazing with intensity boldly looked her up and down.

Her heart almost stopped at the sudden realization that he'd heard her.

She wasn't invisible anymore. He'd seen her! But how?

This wasn't possible.

The sight of his malevolent eyes boring into her sent a shot of panic coursing through her.

Dear God, help me!

As if to confirm her thoughts, he suddenly stepped away from the woman in the chair and started toward her.

Addison froze, her feet glued to the floor. She watched helplessly as he approached. Suddenly he reached out and grabbed her roughly by the arm. A cold she'd never felt before shot through her. She gasped in horror as the man smiled ominously.

"I've been waiting for you," he whispered.

Addison screamed.

"Addison, wake up. Please, wake up!" Kylie demanded as she continued to shake her older sister's shoulders.

Was someone calling to her?

Above her own scream, she heard her name called out.

Addison struggled to calm her rapidly beating heart. To focus on the garbled words that hung heavy in the air just out of reach.

"Addison. You're scaring me!"

She suddenly felt a bright heat hit her face. As if a switch had been flipped, she bolted upright in bed. Sweat dripped down her back. Her heart threatened to rip through her chest. "Where am I?" she muttered.

"Planet Earth last time I checked," Kylie replied in an attempt to lighten the bizarre situation.

"I--I don't understand. What happened?" Addison groaned and immediately shielded her eyes from the sunlight pouring in through her bedroom window. When she finally had a chance to clearly form a cohesive thought, she asked, "Kylie, is that you?"

"Who else would it be in your bedroom?" Kylie's voice wavered. "That must have been a really bad dream."

A dream. Yes, yes, Thank God. It was just a dream.

In an attempt to calm herself, Addison took several deep breaths.

"I wasn't even sure you were sleeping." Kylie leaned in closer to Addison. "You were screaming at the top of your lungs and you had your eyes open."

"What?" Addison slid back against the headboard. She gazed slowly around the room. "That's crazy. I--I couldn't have."

I must have been dreaming. It was so real.

So vivid.

As Addison recalled the dream, the foggy feeling in her head came back. The image of the man with the frightening blue eyes invaded her consciousness.

Suddenly, the hairs on her arms stood up as she looked down at the foot of her bed. She swallowed a scream as she saw him standing there. Leering back at her, sweat prominent on his upper lip.

Jesus! He's there! He's in my bedroom!

Addison grabbed Kylie by the arm. "We've got to get out here before he gets us! Hurry!" She tried to scramble off her bed but in her desperation, she caught her ankle in the covers and almost toppled onto the floor. Kylie grabbed her and pushed her back onto the bed.

"Addison, stop! There's no one here!"

Frantically pointing her trembling finger at the foot of her bed, she stammered, "It's him. It's him. He followed me here!"

"Him who? What are you looking at? There's nobody in here with us."

The man glared at her.

A shiver ran up her spine. Nausea hit her as she found herself unable to move. Unable to breathe.

A sinister laugh erupted in her head.

Addison clasped her hands over her ears.

This isn't real. He isn't real!

She squeezed her eyes shut and bellowed, "Go away. You don't exist!"

Kylie clasped her sister by the shoulders. On the verge of tears, she continued. "What's going on? You're scaring me. Do you want me to get Mom?"

Addison lifted her head and forced herself to look back at the foot of her bed. To her relief, he was gone.

"It was just a dream," Kylie persisted. "A bad nightmare. Honest, there's no one else in here besides you and me."

The fear in Kylie's voice, and her suggestion to get their mother, snapped Addison back to reality. What was she supposed to tell her mother? That she'd had a bad dream and the monster in her dream followed her back to her room? That he stood at the end of her bed, taunting her? Laughing at her?

Kylie reached out and took her sister's hand. "It was a nightmare," she repeated.

Yes, yes, that was it. A nightmare.

She held onto Kylie's words like a life jacket. It was the only thing that made sense. She'd had a stupid nightmare. That's all it was.

"I'd better get Mom."

"No!" Addison cried out as she grabbed her sister and pulled her back onto the bed.

Although she'd like nothing better than to feel the warmth and security of her mother's embrace, she knew Mom had no patience for this sort of thing. She'd simply tell Addison she'd had a bad dream. And she'd be right.

Even if it was the worst dream she'd ever had in her life.

Unwilling to risk her mother's reaction, Addison forced herself to calm down. She regained at least some semblance of self-control. If not for her sake, then for Kylie's. Who at twelve years old was very impressionable.

"No, that's okay. I'm fine, really."

She forced a smile on her face that she didn't quite feel. "Jeez, I must have had a whopper of a dream. I'm sorry I scared you." She let out a little laugh, hoping it wouldn't sound as fake as it felt.

Just then their mother's voice rang out. "Hey, what are you two up to? I thought I heard yelling. Addison, you're not picking on your little sister, are you?"

Addison groaned. "No, Mom."

Kylie chuckled.

"Okay. Just checking." The muffled sound of the downstairs closet door being opened echoed up the stairs. "Kylie, if you want me to drop you off at Laura's, you need to hustle. I don't have time to wait around, or I'll be late for my hair appointment."

Addison looked at Kylie and saw the concerned look on her face. She leaned over and gave Kylie a loving nudge.

"Honestly, I'm fine. I had a bad dream, that's all. It was probably that stupid horror movie Sasha made me watch the other night. I don't know why I let her talk me into watching those things." She pushed aside the covers and swung her feet onto the floor. "Besides, I'm going to head over to the park. Once I get a little fresh air, I'm sure I'll be myself in no time."

Kylie heaved a sigh of relief. "Okay. I bet the air will do you good."

She got up and started from the room when Addison called her back. "Listen, it's probably best if we don't mention this to Mom. You know how she gets."

Her sister nodded. "Sure, no problem."

She watched as Kylie left the room. Wow, her little sister was growing up. It was hard to believe she was only twelve. Some days she seemed wiser beyond her years.

Like today.

The feeling of foolishness she'd felt moments before turned to ridicule. What was wrong with her? How could she have let a stupid dream affect her like that? She wasn't ten years old anymore. Afraid of the boogie man hiding under her bed.

She started to stand up when she felt a sudden painful stinging on her arm. Looking down, she gasped aloud.

The unmistakable red outline of a large hand stood out against her white skin.

In the exact same spot where the orderly had grabbed her.

***

Addison sat in the gazebo in Radley Park. A book was opened in front of her, but her thoughts were elsewhere. She stared down at her arm and ran her fingers lightly over the bruising that was still visible.

Images of that morning crept back in. The memory was so visceral, goose pimples immediately rose on her skin despite the warm temperatures. Once again, she heard the loud cracks of thunder and saw the cold, evil, blue eyes staring back at her.

"Fancy meeting you here."

Addison visibly jumped and shoved her arm in her lap. She'd been so lost in thought she hadn't heard Stan approach.

"Sorry. I didn't mean to startle you," he said as he slid in next to her. "How's it going?" His words faltered as he took a look at her face. "Wow, are you okay? Pardon the pun with everything we're getting into, but it looks like you've seen a ghost."

Without waiting for a response, he dug into the pocket of his jeans, pulled out a thumb drive, and held out his hand. "Here is the copy of the video. Sasha told me I should give it to you to mail out to the contest. Something about you being the responsible one." He dropped the mini USB into the palm of her hand. "I was heading over to your place to deliver it when I saw you sitting here."

Still trying to push the events of the morning to the back of her mind, she closed her hand around the device that suddenly felt heavier than it should.

"Honestly Addison, are you alright? I mean, I know we haven't known each other for that long, but I can tell something isn't right with you."

She thought back to the last time they'd been together. The four friends had sat Indian style in her bedroom, eagerly awaiting Stan to set up his computer so they could watch their video entry. God, was that really only last night? It felt like an eternity ago.

"I--I don't know. It's all so crazy." She heaved a sigh.

"You can tell me anything." He paused. "Think of me as a computer with both software and hardware encryption."

Addison threw him a puzzled look.

He laughed. "Okay. Bad analogy. Instead, how about my lips will be sealed like a vault? You know, as safe as the U.S Treasury's gold bullion at Fort Knox."

She smiled slightly. "How about 'you can trust me'?"

"Yeah, that works too."

Before he'd arrived, she hadn't known what to think. With her thoughts in such turmoil, she'd been confused and frightened. But now, despite his words that made no sense, he was making her feel better. Calmer.

Although she wasn't ready to bare her soul, maybe Stan's logical, scientific opinion was just what she needed.

Slowly and deliberately, she shared the details of her dream. When she was done, she held her arm out. "This is where he grabbed me." She looked at his face and was surprised to see bewilderment.

"Addison, there's nothing there."

Shocked at his words, she looked down at her arm and felt her stomach clench.

The bruising was gone.

"That's impossible," she whispered. "They were there. I just saw them a few minutes ago."

His eyes filled with compassion. "Dreams sometimes do that. They feel so real—"

She angrily jerked her arm back. "It *was* real! I'm not crazy."

"I never said you were."

"But you don't believe me."

"I didn't say that." He took a deep breath and let it out. "Listen, we don't need to do this, you know. We can always tell Sasha and Levi that we've changed our minds."

She gave a sad laugh. "And have the Rage of Sasha fall down on our heads?"

"I'm serious, Addison. We haven't even sent in the video and you're already being tormented in your dreams. And although you haven't come out and said it, I can tell you're not comfortable with being the group psychic. You get a weird look on your face whenever Sasha or Levi bring it up. It's not worth it."

Addison was struck by his words. He was actually willing to give up the chance of being of television because of a nightmare she'd had.

Wow. He really is a nice guy. Like Mom says, maybe chivalry isn't dead.

She shrugged. "There's no guarantee we'll win the contest anyway. Right?"

"Actually, that's a good point. If we factor in all the variables, the probability of our team being selected should be more than a thousand to one."

Addison laughed out loud. Stan may be a little on the dweebie side, but he certainly could change her mood for the better.

"Here's a thought," Stan continued. "Why don't you go visit your Aunt Juliette? Isn't she the one with the otherworldly powers?"

"You've been talking to Sasha, haven't you?"

He smiled. "Yeah, I have. But it makes sense. I bet she would know what to do. I say talk to her. Maybe she can ease your mind."

Addison felt silly for not thinking about confiding in Aunt Juliette in the first place. Maybe talking to Stan was a good idea after all. She patted him on the shoulder before standing up. She tucked the drive safely into her pants pocket, leaned over and picked up her book. She started to walk away, then turned to glance back at him. "You're alright. You know that?"

He beamed in response.

***

"Does your mom know you're here?"

Addison sat at the kitchen table, her eyes glued on the dozens of crystals and dream catchers that surrounded her.

Juliette set down a cup of what looked like dried leaves and twigs in front of Addison before sitting down opposite her.

Addison glanced warily at the cup and tried to unobtrusively push it away.

The older woman reached out and patted her hand. "I know this isn't easy for you."

"I'm sorry you and Mom don't get along. But that shouldn't mean I can't see you when I want to."

Her response was a sad smile. "Are you okay, sweetie? You feel off to me."

Addison knew there was no point in lying to her. Her aunt had an uncanny way of knowing exactly what she was feeling and thinking. Sometimes it was creepy, but right now, it helped start the conversation.

In a halting voice, Addison described the nightmare and the aftermath of seeing the man at the foot of her bed. She then spoke about finding the bruising on her arm. "When I showed it to Stan, it was gone." She shook her head. "I feel like I'm losing my mind."

"Do you know what triggered this?"

She shrugged. "Well, my friends and I are hoping to get on The Ghost Dudes TV show. They're looking for a paranormal investigative team to go out with them on Halloween night."

Juliette raised an eyebrow. "Don't tell me you started your own team."

"Uh, well, yeah."

"Does Anne know about this?"

Addison shook her head. "I doubt we'll even get picked. There's got to be thousands of people applying for this. I figured why get her upset for nothing."

Juliette sighed. "You know the paranormal isn't a game. It needs to be taken very seriously."

"We are taking this seriously."

She abruptly stood up and strode out of the kitchen. A moment later, she returned. In her hand, she held a deck of tarot cards.

"I think we need to look deeper into this."

Addison's eyes widened in astonishment. "Do you think that nightmare was real? Was that guy real?"

"That's what we're about to find out."

She handed Addison the cards and asked her to shuffle them. "When you're done, hand me three cards. We'll do a past, present, and future reading."

Addison did as she asked. After shuffling the deck, she handed her aunt three cards, who placed them face down on the table. Reaching out to her left, Juliette turned over the first card.

"This is in the position of your past. The Three of Cups. This signifies the close friendship and bond that you share with Levi, Sasha and –" She stopped for a moment, then added "—and another who has just joined you. This must be Stan. He's an excellent addition to your group. He's someone you can trust."

She turned over the next card. "This is your present. The Tower represents a leap of faith and delving into the unknown. It also shows a possible journey into the darkness. Things that were hidden may be coming up to the surface." She looked up at her niece. "This could very well be related to your dream.

You've never been someone who enjoys being the center of attention. But now, as the psychic for the group, you'll be front and center. Maybe that's triggering a fear within you that manifested itself in the dream."

"But what about my arm?"

"You said Kylie saw you thrashing about in your bed. Could the bruising have been caused by you unknowingly hitting your nightstand or headboard?"

"But the bruising was in the shape of a hand."

"Kylie grabbed you, didn't she? And if I recall correctly, you were always a kid who bruised easily. We could spit at you and you'd get a huge black and blue."

Addison still wasn't sure. But rather than argue the point, she let it go.

Aunt Juliette's hand hovered over the third card. She turned it over and Addison gasped aloud.

It was the Death card.

"Don't get upset. This is in the position of the future. The Death card doesn't always mean death of the physical body. It can be a death of the way things have been. Nothing is written in stone, Addy. And if you and your friends do win the contest, things will certainly never be the same again."

Addison looked up at her aunt. A sudden feeling came over her that she couldn't explain. But it was too strong to ignore.

She's lying. Aunt Juliette is lying to me.

CHAPTER FOUR

Six Months Later
Halloween Night

"I still can't believe we won. This is too awesome for words!" Levi exclaimed as he swiveled back and forth in the van, determined not to miss anything.

"I told you we'd do it. Your problem is that you just don't have enough faith in us," Sasha retorted.

It was early afternoon on a bright, cool autumn day. The newly formed Ghost Seekers were on their way to the location of their first ever paranormal investigation. They still hadn't been told where they were going, but Sasha, Levi and Stan didn't care. All they cared about was that they'd beat out thousands of other teams for the opportunity to work with The Ghost Dudes.

It was a dream come true.

It hadn't taken much convincing to get their parents to agree to their television debut. Once the friends were informed they'd won, they sat down with their parents, who, since they were all underage, had to sign the contracts allowing them to participate.

Addison's mom and dad were happy she was going to be on TV. They'd always been concerned about her quiet, reserved ways and they felt this was the perfect opportunity for her to break out of her shell and experience the world outside of Millbrook. Although Addison hated doing it, knowing how her mom felt about the paranormal, she made sure to omit that she was the group's psychic. She'd deal with it after the show aired.

Stan's parents were ecstatic that he'd finally made friends. Although they didn't believe in the existence of ghosts, and thought The Ghost Dudes faked everything that happened on their show, they were nevertheless glad to see their son part of a group, regardless of what the group was about.

Levi's parents thought it was funny that their daredevil son was going off ghost-hunting, while Sasha's mother didn't blink an eye. Working two jobs to support the two of them, she simply nodded and signed the paperwork.

Now they were finally on their way to make their television debut.

Levi, who was seated next to Sasha in the second row of seats in the van, leaned over and whispered in her ear, "What do you expect? We don't know squat about ghost investigating."

She waved her brightly colored nails at him. "It's not Einstein, bro," she whispered back. "If worse comes to worse, we'll just imitate whatever The Ghost Dudes are doing. And," she added, leaning in closer, "if you open your big mouth and tell them we're new at this, I'll personally make sure you become a ghost yourself."

Levi sat back and laughed. The laugh froze in his throat when he saw the serious look on her face.

"Man, you Cubans are crazy," he murmured.

"Damn straight."

Addison and Stan sat in the last row of the van. While the three joked and reveled in their good fortune, she remained silent. She wanted so much to be excited. She longed to have the look of happiness that lit up her friends' faces. But no matter how hard she tried, she couldn't get rid of the dread building in the pit of her stomach.

From the moment they heard they'd won the contest, Sasha and the others had spun all sorts of scenarios in which they were famous, drowning in money and being pursued by a legion of hardcore fans. As they laughed and dreamed, Addison grew sicker. And increasingly nervous with each passing day. No matter how hard she tried, she couldn't forget the dream she'd had, or the awful apparition of the evil man standing at the foot of her bed. And no matter what Aunt Juliette said, she didn't believe the bruising on her arm had been caused by Kylie or her own thrashing about. She also couldn't forget the Death Card she'd pulled during her reading with her aunt. Nor the way Aunt Juliette had lied about it. She'd physically felt her aunt's fear. And no explanations about the Death Card meaning positive transformation was going to change that.

Was the dream some kind of warning? Was she foolish not to heed the warning?

Was someone going to die on this investigation?

Now, here she was, seated in a van with her best friends, about to realize their dream of becoming famous. Instead of feeling giddy with excitement, she wanted nothing more than to yell at the van driver to stop so she could get out. The closer the van got to wherever they were going, the more she wanted to escape. She didn't know if she could go through with this, not when every fiber of her being screamed that she should run.

She'd tried several times to broach the subject, but it was pointless. Sasha and Levi were determined not to let anything, especially something as trivial as Addison's fear, deter them from appearing on TV. Stan seemed to be the only one who understood her worry, but the closer they got to the event, the more excited he became.

Glancing out the window at the passing scenery, she sighed. She was trapped. She had no guarantees her dream had been more than just a stupid dream. Maybe it was her imagination working overtime. Maybe her aunt was right. Maybe it was her insecurity about being labeled the group psychic that was making her mind go haywire on her. She knew how much this all meant to them. Was it worth jeopardizing her friendship with people she'd come to care about? Could she honestly screw it up for them because of her own lack of self-confidence?

What a friggin' mess.

She felt a hand gently rest on her arm. Turning, she saw the concerned face of Stan looking back at her.

"You okay? You look as though you're about to lose your lunch. Are you worried about your parents? Did they give you a hard time signing the contract with the network?"

Addison shook her head. "They were cool with it. In fact, they were pretty excited about me being on TV."

"Then what's up?"

"I dunno. Maybe it's meeting The Ghost Dudes, or making an idiot out of myself on camera. I hate having my picture taken. I always think I look like a freak."

Stan gave her a bewildered look. "Addison, that's nuts. You're –" He almost said 'beautiful' but caught himself just in time. Instead, he said, "-- you're very photogenic."

"That's nice of you to say." She tossed her head and smiled at him. "I'll be fine. It's just first-time jitters."

"Probably. Besides, you have nothing to worry about. I'm sure Devon will be hogging up all the camera time."

She chuckled. "Yeah, he does seem to like the spotlight."

"Listen, if you're still worried about being our psychic, make sure you partner up with Tina. Follow her lead and you should be fine."

Surprised at his insight, she was about to respond when Sasha suddenly gasped. "Wow! Will you look at that?"

Addison leaned forward and looked out the windshield. She immediately caught her breath. They were on a long gravel road, bordered on each side by towering evergreens and long-dead oak trees. Although the sun was out, the dense canopy made it feel as though it were dusk. The gnarled gray limbs of the dead trees resembled skeletal fingers beckoning them forward. She gulped as a shot of fear ran down her spine.

Oh my God. This looks like the road I saw from the window in my dream.

"Do you know where we are? Does it look familiar to anyone?" Sasha asked aloud to the group.

Levi shook his head. "Whatever it is, it's certainly creepy. Perfect for Halloween night."

Addison caught a glimpse of rusted wrought iron gates hanging off their hinges as they drove past stone columns that stood on each side of the entrance. There was a name carved on one of the columns, but the van passed too quickly for her to catch it.

The road continued on through what appeared to be a thick forest bordering the road. Addison quickly became aware of a nauseous feeling in the pit of her stomach. She was shocked when she felt a sudden pain in her chest, as if someone had plunged their hand into her ribcage and squeezed her heart in their fist. She'd never felt anything like this before and had no idea what was going on. The feeling of wanting to escape grew stronger until it was all she could do to remain in her seat. Unaware of what she was doing, she reached out and grabbed Stan's hand. He looked at her in surprise and swallowed his yelp as she tightened her grip.

"What's wrong?" he asked.

"My dream," she whispered. "I saw this road and these trees in my dream." She turned her face towards him and he saw the panic in her eyes. "My aunt pulled the Death Card when she did a reading for me. She tried to give me some song and dance about it meaning change. But what if it really means Death? What if someone is going to die here tonight?"

"Addy, calm down. It's going to be fine. We'll watch each other's back the whole night, I promise."

The road curved ahead of them. A few moments later it widened out and they gasped as they came in view of a large five storied, red brick building. It resembled a castle with its looming towers, peaked roofs and tall broken windows, many of which were boarded up. There was an unmistakable air of neglect and abandonment that lent itself to the overall eeriness of the place.

"Holy crap," Sasha said. "What is this place?"

"Welcome to Meadowlark Mental Asylum," the driver replied. "Devon will give you the particulars once we stop."

"Meadowlark Asylum?" Levi asked. "Isn't this in Ashboro?" The van driver nodded.

"I was starting to get weirded out by the winding, isolated dirt roads you took to get us here," Stan admitted. "Really made me feel we were heading to the middle of nowhere."

"I didn't know there was an asylum out here," Sasha spoke up as she pulled out her phone and began to punch in the name onto the internet.

"I remember reading something about it. It was shut down in 1975," Stan explained.

"Why?"

"Nobody knows for sure. One day it was running, and the next the patients were transferred out to other hospitals and the doors were closed."

"There's not much on the internet about this place," Sasha replied. "Just a bit of history of when it was built. There's actually more articles on the town of Ashboro." She read for a few moments before catching her breath. "Wow! Get this. It says here that starting in 1969, a series of disappearances took place in and around both the asylum and the town itself. People began to suspect there was a serial killer on the loose. Police called in the FBI but they couldn't find anything. The disappearances abruptly stopped sometime in late 1972."

"Okay, that just made the creep meter go way up," Levi said.

"Can you imagine? Maybe it was one of the patients sneaking out at night and snatching unsuspecting townspeople!"

Stan frowned. "You actually sound excited about that."

Sasha tossed her head. "I'm excited over the fact that we're going to be investigating a site that may have once housed a real-life serial killer. How friggin' awesome is that? Imagine, coming face to face with Ashboro's version of Jack the Ripper."

He shook his head and glanced at Addison. "I worry about her sometimes," he whispered under his breath.

"There's a bunch of vans already here," Levi pointed out. "I wonder if that means The Ghost Dudes have arrived."

"They've been here since early this morning, setting everything up," the driver explained. He maneuvered the van towards the row of vehicles already parked under the trees.

"Maybe we shouldn't do this," Addison replied softly. The last thing she'd needed to hear was Sasha's announcement about a serial killer loose in the area nearly half a century before. Although she couldn't explain it, Addison had a feeling deep in her gut that the disappearances were somehow related to the building looming up before them. It made her even more desperate to turn around and get the hell out of there.

"Do not go there, Addison," Sasha warned.

"Sasha, this isn't some haunted house. This is an asylum. People probably died here."

"I hate to tell you this, but people die all the time."

"You don't understand..." She tried to explain, but the words caught in her throat.

"Look, it's you who doesn't understand," Sasha said. "The contracts are signed. We're here. How is it going to look if we suddenly back out? The network could sue our parents for breach of contract. Do you want that to happen because you're letting your fears get the best of you?"

Addison tried to tell herself that Sasha was right. Her parents could lose everything they'd spent years building up. With her mother always encouraging her to step out into the world, leave it to her to pick the one occasion that could prove fatal. Despite her body screaming at her to flee, she could see no way out of this.

"Alright," she finally replied. "I won't mention it again."

As they pulled up to a stop, Addison saw two men waiting for them. One had a camera resting on his shoulder, pointed at their arriving van.

"Holy shit! It's Devon Watson," Levi exclaimed, pointing to the other man. "He looks just as he does on TV."

"You think?" Sasha asked. "He looks shorter to me."

She quickly pulled out a compact from her backpack and studied her goth-like make-up for any smears. She'd dyed her hair a bright blue for her television debut and checked to make sure the gel was keeping the short spikes in place.

When the van stopped, the door was pulled open and Devon popped his head in. He was wearing jeans, a white turtleneck sweater and a leather jacket that made him look even more handsome. He smiled and his dazzling white teeth sparkled back at them.

"Hey guys, I'm Devon Watson. Welcome to Meadowlark. You're in for a real treat tonight. This place is going to be spectacular. Now, I'm going to need you to wait one moment while we get the shot set up. We want to capture you guys arriving. So be sure to look excited and eager that you beat out thousands of others to be here. I'll let you know when we're ready."

"I can't believe this is happening," Sasha whispered excitedly. "I'm actually going to be on TV."

"*We're* going to be on TV," Levi corrected her.

"Whatever. The point is we're going to be famous. I can feel it."

Stan and Addison exchanged glances. The only thing Addison felt was the knot growing larger in her stomach.

"Do you want to make a bet that Sasha will be the first to shit herself if we do see a ghost?" Stan joked, trying his best to ease Addison's tension.

It worked. She burst out laughing. At that moment, Devon called from outside the van.

"Okay, guys. We're rolling. Remember, look excited."

The red light came on the camera.

It was showtime.

One by one the four friends exited the van, making sure to ooh and aah at the sight of the building. Devon spoke a few words to each, congratulating them on their win.

Turning towards the camera, he said, "We're here tonight at the infamous Meadowlark Mental Asylum in Ashboro, Massachusetts, surrounded by the beautiful Berkshire Mountains. Built in 1869, it was home to the criminally insane and those unfortunate souls whose echoes have been left behind. When the asylum was closed down forty-four years ago, it wasn't long before rumors and legends began to spring up about the evil that supposedly stalks its halls. Screams and moans are heard on the property, and strange lights are seen in the building that had its electricity turned off decades ago. It's said no one should ever come here after the sun has gone down. Those who have ignored the warnings are never seen again. The locals are convinced they've fallen prey to what they call The Monster of the Asylum. There have also been reports of prior teams coming in to investigate. Unable to speak about what they encountered within the walls behind me, they've never been the same since. We are the first paranormal team to be allowed inside since that fateful night ten years ago, when a team of six Germans entered this building. Before the end of the evening, only five would emerge. Whatever we encounter tonight will be captured live. You'll see what we see. You'll be able to text in to Brandon and let us know if you're seeing something on the monitors that we're not. Tonight, on the evening when the veil is the thinnest between the world of the living and the world of the dead, you'll have an opportunity to investigate right alongside us." He paused, then arched his eyebrow dramatically. "If you dare."

Addison gave a start and quickly looked to her friends. Caught up in Devon's words, she couldn't believe that Sasha and Levi looked even more excited. She glanced at Stan and saw him giving her an encouraging smile.

"Cut," Devon called out. "That was great, guys. You're naturals in front of the camera."

He started to walk away when Addison blurted out, "What do you mean only five emerged? A paranormal investigator *died* here?"

"Yeah. Rad, right?"

Addison was stunned by his response. "How is that rad? A person lost their life in there during an investigation and now you expect us to spend the night?"

A look of impatience flashed over Devon's face before it was replaced by his megawatt smile. "Listen sweetheart, you and your friends signed up for this. What did you think this was going to be? A walk through Disney World?"

"No, but—"

"We were flooded with entries. Thousands would love to be standing where you are. So be a good girl and just smile at the camera. We'll take care of the rest."

Anger surged through Addison. She despised his condescending attitude. She opened her mouth to protest, but was interrupted when Tina Landry came up.

"Hey, you must be Addison," she greeted. "I remember you from your video. You're the team psychic."

Still upset, Addison gave a quick nod. Tina leaned in and whispered, "Devon can be an ass sometimes. Just ignore him. I've learned to." She took a step back and introduced herself to the others. "I love your name. The Ghost Seekers. It's very catchy. Sasha, Levi, why don't you go over and introduce yourselves to Mark? You can compare notes on capturing EVPs and photographs. Stan, I'm sure you're going to want to talk to Brandon about setting up basecamp. He's over there by the first van. Addison, you come along with me. I'd like to show you around a bit." She linked her arm with Addison's and pulled her away from the group. Soon they were strolling along the front of the building. "I always get yelled at for doing this, but I like to familiarize myself with an area before it gets dark. Naturally I save whatever psychic impressions I get for the camera."

As they walked along, Tina chitchatted about her life and how she'd come to be on The Ghost Dudes. Addison found she liked the young woman and tried to listen to the conversation. However, with each step, she felt the pain in her chest growing sharper as her stomach continued to clench.

Maybe I'm having a heart attack. At least whatever is inside this building won't be killing me.

As Tina continued speaking, Addison felt increasingly uneasy. She couldn't quite put her finger on what it was that had her so nervous. Suddenly it hit her. She came to a stop and pointed towards the woods.

"Do you hear that?"

Tina, who was taken aback by Addison's abrupt actions, looked towards the woods.

"What am I supposed to be hearing?"

"Birds. Or some kind of wildlife. But there's nothing. There are no sounds at all."

Tina turned back to her. "Maybe the activity of the crew has them spooked."

"You don't think it's *too* quiet?"

Tina thought for a moment, then shook her head.

Addison started to protest, but at the last minute, decided it was best to keep her mouth shut. If Tina wasn't unsettled by the eerie silence, there wasn't anything she could say that would convince her otherwise. She turned back towards the building and looked up at the windows looming overhead. They were all boarded up except for one. Addison gasped when she saw a shadow dart by inside, its image reflected in the grime of the glass.

"What's wrong now?" Tina asked.

"I thought I saw something up there," Addison replied.

Tina looked up to where Addison pointed. "It's probably one of the cameramen setting up the equipment. They're all over inside, making sure everything is ready for us to begin the investigation. Because it's live, it's going to be a little trickier than usual."

Addison nodded, but for reasons she couldn't quite understand, Tina's words didn't ring true.

"So, tell me about yourself. How did you and your friends come to form The Ghost Seekers?"

Just as Addison began to describe the day Sasha appeared with the newspaper ad, Tina's cellphone rang. She slipped it out of her jacket pocket and glanced at it.

"I have to take this. I'll just be a sec." She stepped away and answered. She listened for a few moments, then exclaimed in a frustrated voice, "What do you mean you can't find it? I thought I left it on my bureau. Are you sure you've checked everywhere?"

Standing alone, Addison looked around at the woods surrounding them. Her gaze rested on an especially old oak tree, its' branches gnarled and bent with age. Suddenly, the tree disappeared, and Addison saw a gold half heart pendant with the word MOM engraved on it dancing before her eyes. It was so vivid, it took her breath away. Information flooded into her brain and before she could stop herself, she grabbed Tina and pulled her towards the line of vans.

"What are you doing?" Tina asked, disconcerted by Addison's actions.

"Your pendant. It fell between the seats in your van."

"What?"

"Your half heart pendant. The one you lost. It's not in your apartment. It's in the van."

Tina stared at her in astonishment. "I gotta go," she said into the phone before hanging up.

Dumbfounded, she allowed the teenager to lead her towards a blue van that was parked in the middle of the row. When they arrived, Addison pointed to it.

"You drove here in this van, right?" Tina nodded. "Your pendant is wedged between the last row of seats."

Astounded by what Addison was telling her and curious to see if she was right, Tina opened the van and climbed inside. A moment later, she emerged, the pendant dangling from her hand.

"How did you know it was there?" she asked. "How did you even know I'd lost a pendant? I never said what I'd lost when I was talking to my roommate on the phone just now."

"I don't know. I just did."

Tina's eyes narrowed as she studied the teenager. "How long have you been a psychic?"

Addison looked away, uncomfortable under Tina's gaze. "I'm not sure I am one. It must have been a lucky guess." She looked across the lawn. "I think Sasha is looking for me. I'll see you over by the entrance."

She hurried away, leaving behind a concerned Tina. Since arriving earlier in the day, she'd been feeling an underlying darkness to the property they were about to investigate. If what she'd just witnessed was any indication of Addison's abilities, she worried how the teenager was going to fare as the evening progressed.

"If you're not a sensitive, I'm Beyonce," she murmured under her breath.

***

"That girl is one powerful psychic."

Fifteen minutes after the episode with Addison, Tina had found Mark and pulled him beneath one of the oaks far enough away from the crew to ensure privacy.

"What are you talking about?" Mark responded. She described the incident with the pendant. "Maybe it was a lucky guess."

"That's what she said. But she never heard me tell my roommate what I'd lost. Nor could she have known what van I arrived in or where I was seated in the van."

"So what are you telling me?"

"Ever since Devon and the network decided we were going to investigate Meadowlark Asylum, I've been getting a bad feeling about it. There's something here that feels completely off."

"That's good. That means we'll be sure to capture something tonight."

She gave him an angry look. "Don't you get it? We've got a bunch of kids with us, one of whom is obviously extremely gifted. This could go wrong is so many different ways." She pulled her hand through her hair. "I knew Devon was wrong in picking a group of teenagers to investigate with us."

"He needed to make sure they could be easily—" Mark abruptly stopped speaking

"Say it, Mark. He needed to make sure they could be easily manipulated." He stared uncomfortably at the ground. "But this is different. There's something in that building that's dark. We can't let a group of young people stumble around in there. What if something happens to them? Will you be able to live with yourself if one of them gets hurt or, God forbid, dies?"

Mark rolled his eyes. "Tina, stop being such a drama queen. We've never had one accident or death in the five years you've been with us. The most dangerous areas have already been cordoned off. We're just going to be investigating the basement and the second and third floors which were thoroughly checked out for safety before we even arrived. The kids will always have one of us along, so they're not going to be alone. Besides, Devon has set up some stuff that is sure to wow the audience and bring those ratings up."

"Ratings are one thing. Our lives are another."

He put his hand on her shoulder. "Don't wreck this, Tina. This means as much to you as it does to us. We just need to make it through tonight. That's all. In fact, Devon confided in me on the way down that we're this close to being booked on one of the late night talk shows. We'll be the first paranormal group to do that. It all hinges on how we do tonight. Think about that before you make a stink."

He walked away, leaving a fuming Tina. What did she expect? Mark always took Devon's side in everything. It was as though he'd been born with absolutely no backbone.

She glanced up at the building and sighed.

Appearing on a late night talk show? Actually, that would be pretty special. She could picture herself sitting in the same chair some of her favorite actors and singers have sat in. She allowed her mind to drift away as she thought about the style of dress she'd wear. Should she wear something classy? With lots of bling? Or something a bit sexy that would show off her well-toned figure, or should she --

Tina suddenly caught her breath. She narrowed her eyes, but whatever she'd seen in the large rectangular window was gone. Looking back to the vans, she took count and saw that all the cameramen were on the lawn, along with Mark, Devon and the teenagers.

What had she just seen? Was it what Addison had seen earlier?

Her euphoria over going on late night disappeared, replaced by a sinking feeling in the pit of her stomach.

God, what have we gotten ourselves into?

***

In an effort to gain control over her growing fear and uneasiness, Addison wandered towards a small grove of trees away from the activity nearer to the building. She was angry at herself for telling Tina about her pendant. It only made her look as though she was showing off, though that had never been her intention.

Why couldn't I have just kept my big mouth shut?

She knew once she stepped inside the asylum, she'd be on the go the whole time. Not to mention having a camera shoved constantly in her face. Snatching a few moments of silence under these trees was her only chance to regain some kind of balance before it was show time.

The sun was starting its descent. At this time of year, night came early. The clearing under the trees looked dark and a bit gloomy, but it was perfect for what Addison needed to do. Her aunt had taught her a technique to help re-center herself. If there was ever a time she needed to feel back in balance, it was now.

She spied a spot beneath an old oak that looked perfect. She started towards it, only to stop when she felt herself step on something squishy. She looked down and in the dimming light, uttered a gasp.

A dead crow lay at her feet.

Addison jerked her head up and gazed at her surroundings. She felt nauseous when for the first time, she noticed a mound of dead crows piled under the tree.

"What the—" she whispered under her breath. Terrified of the sight of so many dead birds and not knowing why they were there, she turned on her heel and ran back to the group just as Devon came towards them.

"Okay, we're about to start—"

"There's a pile of dead crows under that tree over there!" Addison cried out as she dashed up to her friends.

"Nice," Devon replied dismissively.

"But why are they there? What happened to them?" she persisted.

Devon took a deep breath and let it out slowly as the four teenagers turned and stared at him. He held his hands up.

"I can't say I understand it, but from what we were told, there's some sort of energy vortex over this building that knocks birds out of the sky when they attempt to fly over."

"But there are so many!"

"The crew gathered them up and placed the majority of them over there. We didn't want to be stepping on them."

"You missed a few," Stan said as he pointed towards one of the cameramen filming Mark commenting of the few remaining crows left on the lawn.

"That's disgusting!" Addison cried out, her voice notably higher with fear.

Devon took another steadying breath and let it out slowly.

Christ, I hope she's not going to be a pain in my ass tonight. What is it with psychics? First Drama Queen Tina, now this kid.

Walking up to her, he placed his hand on her shoulder and fixed what he hoped was a sorrowful expression on his face. "I agree. It's horrible. I hate to see any kind of animal or bird hurt in any way. But there's nothing we can do to help them. Now I need you to calm yourself. We're about to film our entry into the asylum. Okay?"

The last thing Addison wanted to say was okay. This was *not* okay. Didn't they understand what was happening? The building was *killing* birds! What the hell was it going to do to *them?*

Sasha came up beside her. "We can do this, Addy. I'll be next to you every step of the way."

"Me too," Stan said.

"And me," Levi agreed.

She looked to each of them before reluctantly nodding. "Okay, Devon."

"Perfect! Let's go over to the front steps where Todd will be filming. As we each enter, I don't want you to look frightened. I want you to look concerned. After all, this place has a bad reputation and you're about to walk inside. But you're ghost hunters. You may be worried, but you're also brave. The audience needs to see your courage. Also, be careful of all the wires. This place hasn't seen electricity for years so we needed to plug in all our equipment to several generators we brought with us." He smiled. "We don't want your television debut to involve tripping over a wire and falling flat on your face." He clapped his hands. "Let's do this."

With the cameras rolling, Devon and Mark entered. Tina, Sasha and Levi fixed their best concerned look on their faces and followed. Stan paused. Instead of looking concerned, he theatrically threw his shoulders back, put on a grin that announced to the audience that he wasn't afraid of anything and entered.

It was now Addison's turn. She'd be damned if she pretended to feel something she wasn't. With a stony expression on her face and her mouth set in a grim line, she climbed the stairs. Just as she was about to enter, she suddenly felt dizzy and off balance. She lowered her gaze and was shocked to hear the loud crashing of thunder roaring around her.

She had a sense of hands reaching out to her. A moment later, she heard a rasping whisper in her ear.

I'm waiting for you.

Rattled, she turned to see the cameraman gesturing frantically to her to go inside. But she couldn't.

You can't. You can't go in there! You'll never come out if you do.

She wanted, needed to run. She had to escape the madness waiting for her inside.

Screw the show. Screw everything. She wanted to live.

Just as she was about to turn and dash back down the stairs, Sasha, Levi and Stan appeared in the doorway just out of camera range. They gestured at her to come inside. Stan in particular waved at her to enter.

It'll be okay, he mouthed to her.

It won't be okay. But I can't leave you all inside. You all have been there for me. Now I need to be there for you, if only to make sure you all survive.

With her heart pounding loudly in her ears and in her chest, she took a deep breath.

"Please God, help me," she whispered. Then she stepped inside.

CHAPTER FIVE

Addison caught her breath as she stepped into the foyer. Although it was late October and the night was chilly, the inside of the asylum was freezing. There had to be at least a twenty-degree difference in temperature. In spite of the coat, scarf, and gloves she wore, she nevertheless shivered and crossed her arms tightly against her chest.

"Did we just walk into a refrigerator?" Stan whispered as he came up next to her. She nodded in response.

"Okay team, listen up," Devon called out as he led everyone from the entryway through a set of paint-chipped double doors, and into the first room on the right. "This is basecamp."

Waving his hand, he continued walking towards the back of what may have once been a waiting room of sorts. Several large cables were duct taped to the floor, all leading towards an array of monitors sitting on a long, flat table. Carefully stepping over the wires, Devon guided the group towards a man on his hands and knees who was plugging in the last of the monitors. "Everybody, this is our computer guru, Brandon Middleton. Brandon, you already met Stan outside. Say hello to the rest of our winning team."

The man quickly finished what he was doing before getting to his feet and turning towards them. "So this is the group I've heard so much about. Great job on your video, by the way." Brandon wiped his dust-ridden palms on his jeans before reaching out and shaking each of the teenagers' hands. Starting with Levi, he said, "Let me see if I remember correctly. Levi, right?"

"Yes, sir."

"Sir?" Brandon laughed out loud. "No need to call me sir. You make me feel old. You do what Mark does, correct? You're the EVP expert." Levi slowly nodded, suddenly nervous to be called an expert on something he'd never done before.

"You're Sasha," Brandon said next. "You're the team photographer. I'd love to see some of your work when this investigation is over." If Sasha was worried over showing him photographs she didn't have, she never showed it. He smiled at Stan. "As I said to you earlier, I'm looking forward to working with you tonight, Stan."

"The name is Razor, remember?"

Brandon lifted a bemused eyebrow as he caught Sasha rolling her eyes in disgust. "Sure, Razor. Sorry. When I'm setting up equipment, I have a tendency to forget everything."

"No problem," Stan replied.

When Brandon turned to Addison, he paused for a long moment before giving her an odd smile. "And you must be the psychic. Welcome, Addison."

"Nice to meet you," Addison replied, suddenly anxious over his strange behavior. He was looking at her as if she had two heads. Which was weird. He must know all about psychics; he worked closely with Tina.

A thought occurred to her that sent a shot of fear rushing through her. Was he acting that way because he knew she had no experience being a psychic? Did he think she was a fake?

Brandon continued to give her an appraising look, unaware of the turmoil his behavior was causing in the young teenager.

You guys have no idea what you're in for. Especially you, Addison. Devon will make sure of that.

"I hope you all have on your grown up panties," he finally

exclaimed. "Tonight promises to be one hell of a ride."

Sasha, Levi and Stan cheered, while Addison remained quiet.

Standing off to the side, Tina took in the display. She noticed how pale Addison looked. Compared to her friends' reactions, the poor girl looked as though she wanted to be anywhere but here. It was true the building was throwing off a peculiar vibe, but if she was already afraid of her own shadow before they'd even started their investigation, how was she going to make it through the night? Would she? Or would she end up bagging out on them? Would that be such a bad thing? Ratings would shoot through the roof if the audience thought one of the psychics was so scared of the place, they'd had to leave.

Tina recoiled as she realized what she was thinking. My God, she thought. I'm getting as bad as Devon.

Once again, she felt her anger and frustration returning. This time, however, instead of her ire being directed at Devon's condescending behavior towards her, it was directed at herself. No matter how much she wanted to deny it, the truth was that she'd made a pact with the devil. In exchange for allowing herself to be pulled into situations she didn't feel comfortable in, or having her abilities disregarded by Devon and Mark, she stayed because she had as much at stake as the others. She was just as concerned about the ratings as her team members were. She'd allowed the fame to seduce her.

And that made her uneasy.

How far was she willing to jeopardize her safety to stay on TV? How often was she willing to ignore the alarms bells going off within that warned her to get as far away from Meadowlark Asylum as possible?

Her eyes strayed back to Addison. Was that why she looked so pale and unsettled? Was she stuck in a situation that she could find no way out of?

Maybe we're more alike than I thought.

Whatever it was, Tina decided to keep an eye on Addison throughout the evening. She swore to herself that at the first sign of trouble, TV show or no TV show, she was grabbing the teenagers and getting out of that building as quickly as possible.

We just need to get through this one night. Just twelve more hours.

"We're about to get the cameras rolling again," Devon announced. "Before we do, let's go over a couple of things. We're going to start the investigation by going out in teams. That will allow us to get the lay of the land so we don't become lost when we go out alone later on in the evening."

"Alone?" Addison asked, the fear evident in her voice.

"Don't worry. When I say alone, you won't really be alone. Each of you will be accompanied by a cameraman at all times. Remember, this is a live broadcast. Whatever you do, the audience will see it. And not to make you any more nervous than you may already be, we've got over three million people watching us tonight. Therefore, be professional. But if you see, feel, or hear anything, don't hold back. If you're excited, show it. If you're scared, show it. We want the audience to feel as though they're right next to us."

One of the two man camera crew raised his hand high in the air, then said, "Ready in three, two, one." He pointed at Devon.

"We're back!" Devon said, facing the camera lens. "Make sure you stay tuned tonight to experience the ride of your life!" He laughed, exaggerating his smile. "Since it's impossible for you to physically be here with us, you are going to experience the next best thing. You will be walking hand in hand with us on a virtual tour as we investigate the infamous and, some say, evil Meadowlark Asylum."

Tina remained standing in the shadows, happy to let Devon be the star. Although there were times lately that the man made her skin crawl, she couldn't deny he certainly knew how to put on a show.

"We're going to approach this investigation a little differently. As you may recall from our previous shows, Tina, Mark and I investigate as a team, while Brandon here," Devon said, glancing over his shoulder, then back to the camera, "mans basecamp. Tonight, since we have the Ghost Seekers with us, we are going to split up into groups. Levi, you and Sasha will be with me. Stan, since you're the computer whiz, you'll hang here with Brandon. Tina, just to make things interesting, you and Addison will go with Reggie and do a cursory walkthrough to see what, if any, psychic impressions you get."

Tina cursed under her breath. What was he doing? They'd discussed having two groups go out, each with their own psychic. He'd never mentioned she and Addison going out together with only a cameraman in tow. What kind of game was Devon playing?

As if reading her mind, he spoke to the audience. "Sometimes I like to think outside the box. And this is one of those times." He paused for effect. "Just think, you'll have the rare opportunity to experience the chills and thrills of two psychics as they walk through a haunted asylum on All Hallows Eve. Alone. Without EMF meters, without recorders. Actually, without any electronics at all." His grin widened, "Well, with the exception of the camera, that is."

Reggie panned the camera on Tina, who struggled to put a smile on her face, even as her insides boiled with anger.

Calm down. This is what Devon wants. Do not give him the satisfaction of watching you lose it on camera. Just get through the show. You can kill him afterwards.

The thought of wrapping her hands around his throat lit up her face and changed her smile from a fake one to a heartfelt one.

***

Tina and Addison walked down the main corridor with Reggie close at their heels. With the hallways bathed in darkness, the bright light of the camera shining from behind, as well as the flashlight each woman held, became the only light guiding their way.

Their lights revealed the years of neglect. Wooden slats poked through missing layers of horse hair plaster, while the floor lay in a heavy carpet of dust. Cobwebs stretched from the broken brass lanterns dangling precariously from the wall. Tina grimaced at the thought of all those cobwebs.

God, I hate spiders.

"Addison, be careful where you walk," she said in a carefully measured voice that hid the fear churning inside. "I don't want to see you trip on something."

"Sure."

Noticing how quiet Addison had become since leaving basecamp, Tina felt the pressure of trying to get the girl to talk, if only for the audience at home.

"Are you picking up anything yet?"

"No."

"How about your senses? Are you experiencing any strange emotions, you know, something you didn't feel a moment ago?"

"Uh uh."

Dear God! It's like pulling teeth with this girl.

She came up beside Addison and tugged at her sleeve. "Hey Addison," she whispered. "Is everything okay? You're awfully quiet."

Tina was surprised to feel Addison's body go rigid. *What is going on here?*

She glanced at her and was startled to see a blank look on the girl's face. Where had that come from? She'd been fine a second ago. Damn it! What was wrong with her? The last thing they needed was the audience turning off the show because Addison was as exciting as a cardboard box. They needed to do something to liven things up. And fast.

Unfortunately, Addison was forcing her to rely on one of Devon's fake set-ups. She loathed doing it, but she needed to get the audience and Addison involved before the people at home completely lost interest.

"A few doors down to the right is where I believe the library was located," Tina explained. "There's been reports of strange lights moving past the windows at night. Let's go check it out."

No response from Addison.

Tina and Reggie exchanged glances. The cameraman jerked his head towards the library, and she nodded.

They were just reaching the entrance when Tina heard a low moan. Turning to her right, she was surprised to see it had come from Addison. What in heaven's name was she up to? Was she actually playing to the camera? Was she faking her behavior to garner some sort of attention?

Not sure what to do, Tina gently took Addison by the elbow. Turning to face Reggie, with the camera still rolling, she spoke to the audience and Addison at the same time. "Are you okay?"

No response.

With her frustration mounting, she pulled Addison along. "Come on, let's go into the library."

Still no reaction.

By now ready to strangle the young woman, Tina was about to pinch her in desperation when Addison suddenly jerked her arm free from Tina's grasp. Turning on her heel, she hurried down the corridor, disappearing into the darkness.

Tina's mouth dropped open in shock. "Addison, what are you doing? Get back here now!"

She swung her flashlight in the direction Addison had taken. To her dismay, the corridor was empty.

"What the –?"

Tina caught herself before she uttered the curse word.

"She can't be far," Reggie replied from behind the camera. "She must have ducked into one of the rooms."

"Let's check them out then. We can't have one of our psychics disappearing on us, now can we?"

Although she tried to sound as though she were joking, an edge crept into her words. With her temper growing, Tina turned and did the only thing she could do under the circumstances. She followed Addison down the dark corridor.

***

"Let's review before we head out," Devon announced. Levi, Sasha and Stan stopped chatting amongst themselves and sat up, awaiting his words as if he were a prophet come to save them.

This is how it should be, Devon thought to himself. He'd been right about these kids. They were like putty in his hands, just waiting to be molded. And coerced to do and say whatever he wanted. Tonight was going to be outstanding, he just knew it!

"Since the state authorities have graciously allowed us to enter this building after shutting it down ten years ago, we have to obey a few safety rules." He paused to heighten the tension and inwardly smiled when he saw the teenagers lean towards him. "Do you recall my bit on camera when I told the audience about the German crew that had investigated here?"

Stan was the first to speak up. "How could we forget? Six came in and only five emerged. Right?"

"Exactly Stan. You're a sharp kid."

"That's why they call me Razor."

Sasha and Levi rolled their eyes, while Devon snorted. "Oh yeah. Right."

Ignoring Stan's request to be called Razor, Levi asked, "Can you tell us what happened to him?"

"He didn't listen to the safety rules. I'll go into more detail at the show's finale, when we wrap up the investigation. Since you guys are new to show business, I'll let you in on a little secret. You always end with a *bang!* If you tease your audience with a cliffhanger, it'll leave them always wanting more."

Devon grinned when he saw them all smile and nod eagerly in response. God, he had these kids already eating out of his hand. Could it really be this easy?

"Do you mind if I ask a question?" Stan piped up.

"Shoot."

"Earlier, you mentioned something about 'The Monster of the Asylum.' And about other teams possibly going insane when they investigated here. What was that all about?"

"That's actually two questions." When Stan gave him a stony look, he waved him off with a laugh. "Don't worry about it. Like I said, all that will come out in the big reveal at the end of the show." His smile widened. "You wouldn't want me planting too many pre-conceived notions in your minds before we begin our investigation, would you? You need to keep open minds if this evening is to be a success. Everything must be on the up and up." Devon's own words sounded funny, even to him. It was all he could do to stifle a laugh.

Yup, on the up and up. That was friggin' hilarious. I'm getting really good at this. So good in fact that I almost convinced myself of my sincerity.

"Now, let's get a move on. Our audience is expecting to be *wowed*!"

***

Addison felt as though she'd just awakened from a restless nap. Her head was heavy, and she felt a slight headache at the edges of her consciousness. Rubbing her temples with her fingertips in an attempt to loosen the cobwebs, she finally felt her mind start to clear. She looked around and her blood instantly ran cold. Where was she? The last she remembered, she'd been walking down the corridor with Tina and Reggie. Now she was standing all alone in a dark, dust-ridden, abandoned room.

What the hell happened?

Her heart almost stopped when she heard the shuffling of feet. Whirling around and shining her flashlight out in front of her, she almost cried with relief when she saw Tina and Reggie appear at the door.

"Addison, what are you doing? You can't just walk off like that!" Tina scolded.

"I'm sorry. I don't know what happened. I just –"

Suddenly, Tina and Reggie felt very far away, even though they were standing only inches from Addison. The room went very still, the only sound the beating of her heart in her ears.

Terrified, but unable to stop herself, Addison slowly turned around and scanned her surroundings with the flashlight. Hanging haphazardly from the wall, attached to the remnants of cracked ceramic tiles, was an array of white metal cabinets. Some were dented and marred by rust, while others held what looked like decaying yellowed pieces of paper. Here and there, tiny shards of glass sparkled in the beam of the flashlight.

Beneath the cabinets, tucked into the corner of the room lay a six-foot metal bed. Three large wheel-like handles protruded out from beneath its surface, while bits of dried leather, and a large rusted buckle hung lifelessly to its side.

A shiver ran up Addison's spine at the sudden realization of the pain that was inflicted on the poor souls that had met their fate in this room.

Tina's voice crashed into her daze-like state. "Addison, why in God's name did you come in here of all places? You realize this was the old operating room, don't you?"

Just as Addison opened her mouth to respond, she felt a

strange sensation come over her. Her head suddenly felt dense. Heavy again. "I—I don't know what's happening." Her words lay thick on her tongue as she struggled to make sense of what she was saying. Had she spoken? She wasn't sure. Her thoughts suddenly felt as impenetrable as a wad of cotton.

As she struggled to make sense of what was happening to her, she suddenly heard low guttural laughter coming from the right side of the room.

I told you I was waiting for you.

It was the same voice she'd heard when she'd entered the building. The same voice that had tortured her in her nightmare.

Oh my God! It can't be!

She opened her mouth to scream, but nothing came out. She felt the need to run. To escape this horrible place. It truly was a place of madness, and it was dragging her down into its own depths of hell.

To her horror, she found herself walking towards the sound. She struggled to free herself from whatever pushed her forward, but it was useless. She had no power over her own body.

Her mind shrieked in desperate fear as she watched a shadow begin to materialize before her. Unable to stop what was happening, she raised her hand and pointed to the shadow. She whispered, "Tina. Do you see that?"

"Addison, what are you talking about? Look at what?" Tina reached out to grab Addison by the arm, but she was too late. Addison eluded her grasp and moved towards the far right-hand corner of the room. "Where are you going? What's wrong with you? Get back here, now!"

Addison's eyelids grew heavy as her mind became encased in a fog she couldn't escape. The shadow grew sharper the nearer she drew to it. She could just make out the figure of a man standing in the corner with his back to her. Her senses begged her to stop. To turn around. To run. But whatever pushed her forward was stronger. She felt like a puppet, with someone else – someone she couldn't see pulling the strings. She had no choice but to walk up to the shadow. To move past him until they were facing each other.

Against her will, Addison slowly lifted her eyes. And gasped aloud as the shadow's face became clearer. She stared in helpless horror at the tortured anguish disfiguring his features. At his mouth wide open in a soundless scream of torment and suffering.

His hand came up, his skeletal fingers wrapping themselves tightly around her wrist. Feeling his cold, deadly grip against her skin, the spell was broken. Addison shook off the fog and screamed.

Knees buckling beneath her, she fell to the floor.

CHAPTER SIX

"Be careful here. We don't need anyone getting hurt."

Sasha and Levi were following Devon down a dark, derelict corridor. Rooms opened out on either side, some with doors, some without. The walls and ceilings were peeling with white paint and the floor was covered in a thick carpet of dust, broken plaster and the occasional abandoned chair.

While Tina, Reggie and Addison were doing their walk about on the third floor, Sasha, Levi, Devon and their cameraman Todd were investigating the long corridor on the second floor. They were barely into their walk when it became obvious that the twenty-eight-year-old Todd thought Sasha was hot, taking every opportunity when Devon wasn't looking to point the camera at her.

Sasha ate it up. It took every ounce of willpower not to keep looking at Todd, or rather, Todd's camera. She had to admit, he was kinda cute, though a little too thin for her taste. And there was no way she'd be caught dead dating a guy whose hairline was receding. Still, mindful of Devon's instructions to look and act professional, she had to force herself to refrain from mugging at the camera.

"Where exactly are we?" Levi asked as he held the recorder tightly in his hand.

"We're in the main corridor that runs the length of the asylum," Devon explained. "The point where we started was where the administrative offices were located. Where we are now is the beginning of the patients' rooms."

Levi stuck his head into one of the rooms and saw a metal bed frame leaning upright against the wall. There was a chair lying upside down next to it. The room was small, and it looked so bare and forlorn, he shuddered at the thought of someone being confined in there.

"These rooms are where the cooperative patients were kept," Devon continued. "The further down the corridor you go is where the more, shall we say, difficult patients were housed."

"What about the criminally insane? They weren't kept down here, were they?" Sasha asked.

"They were isolated up on the top floor. For obvious reasons, they needed to be kept separate from everyone else."

The two teenagers had seen enough horror movies set in mental asylums to conjure up all sorts of horrifying images in their imaginations. They constantly looked around them, almost expecting something or someone to jump out at them.

"Did they keep kids here?" Levi asked.

"Sadly, yes. You need to remember that back in the 1800s, families had the ability to commit those they found troublesome and difficult to handle. And in the early 20th Century, there weren't a lot of choices where to place children who exhibited what their doctors considered psychotic behavior."

"That's sick," Sasha exclaimed.

"This was before the days of laws protecting the more vulnerable members of society."

"That still doesn't make it right," she insisted.

In order to diffuse her growing indignity, Devon replied, "Sasha, I'm sure the audience would like to hear about your most interesting investigation. Why don't you tell us about it?"

She and Levi froze. He gave her a panicked look which instantly disappeared when she glared a warning at him. They'd been careful so far not to let on that this was their first investigation. Levi's deer in the headlights look was sure to give them away. Having exaggerated their experience on their audition tape, they now had to live up to their hype.

On live TV.

"Gee Devon, it's hard to narrow it down," Sasha answered with a bravado that left Levi admiring her ability to think on the spot.

"There must be something you can share with our viewers."

Mindful of the camera pointed at her, Sasha tilted her head to one side and tried to look as though she were deep in thought. "Well, let's see. There was the time we had a couple call us in because they kept hearing furniture moving around in their house after they'd gone to bed. The wife started sleepwalking, which was weird cos she'd never done that before. So we set up cameras throughout the house, including their bedroom to see if we could capture any of the activity."

"And did you?"

"I'll say we did. We actually saw the blankets pulled off them by unseen hands. The creepiest part is when the camera showed the wife standing over the sleeping husband for hours, just staring at him. It was like she was in some sort of a trance. We did some research and were able to uncover that her family had been involved with some stuff you shouldn't get involved with, like Ouija boards and seances. Yeah, I'd say that was probably our most interesting case. Right, Levi?"

She turned to him and was surprised to see the panicked look back on his face. She gave him another withering glance.

"Uh yeah, sure. That was interesting."

She rolled her eyes. God, he sounded so lame.

"Todd, let's check out this room," Devon announced as he and the cameraman went into a room to their left.

"What is your problem?" Sasha whispered once she and Levi were alone. "You're acting like a complete dweeb. And stop looking so terrified. You're making it look like this is our first investigation."

"It *is* our first investigation, and of course I'm terrified!" Levi answered. "You just gave Devon the entire plotline of the movie *Paranormal Activity*!"

"I did? Huh. No wonder it sounded familiar."

"Sasha! Levi! Remember what I said. We stay together no matter what!" Devon called out from inside the room.

"We can't show we don't know jack," Sasha continued. "So stop gripping the recorder like it's a life preserver, and pretend you know what you're doing." She turned around. "Coming, Devon!"

She quickly disappeared into the room, leaving a nervous Levi.

"Dammit. I sucked at theatre arts," he muttered before he hurried along after her.

They found themselves standing in a room that was slightly larger than the bedrooms they'd been passing. Instead of a bed frame, this one had the remains of a desk and old metal cabinets whose empty drawers were strewn haphazardly on the floor.

"This was the office of the head nurse," Devon said to the camera. "From here she could keep an eye, not only on the patients, but on her staff as well."

He walked around the room and placed himself behind the wooden desk that was missing one leg, leaving it sloping to the left.

"Levi, why don't you begin an EVP session after Sasha takes some photographs?"

Sasha lifted her camera and snapped off several shots. When she was done, Devon nodded to Levi. Determined not to show that he had no clue what he was doing, Levi lifted the recorder and tried his best to recall how Mark did his recordings on The Ghost Dudes TV program.

"EVP session with Devon, Sasha, Todd and myself. It's 7:30 pm and we're standing in the head nurse's office on the second floor of the Meadowlark Mental Asylum. Is there anyone here who wishes to communicate with us? You can speak into this machine I have in my hand. The red light is on which means you can say whatever you want. You can start off by telling us your name."

They all waited expectantly.

"Don't be shy," Levi said again. "Please tell us if there's anyone in here with us."

The thick silence grew. Just as Levi was about to start begging, the air was suddenly filled with the sound of faint music. A moment later, the scratchy music was accompanied by the high pitched, nasal voice of a male singer.

"Oh my God!" Devon exclaimed. "Are you guys hearing that?" Levi and Sasha nodded vigorously, their eyes wide with astonishment as they looked about. "Wow, this is weird. If I'm not mistaken, it sounds like a recording of Vagabond Lover by Rudy Vallee."

"Who?" Sasha asked.

"He was a huge recording star in the 1920s and 30s."

The music abruptly stopped, leaving the group staring at each other in wonderment.

"But why would that music be playing here?" Levi questioned.

Devon withdrew a piece of paper from his jacket and held it up to the camera. It was black and white and showed a middle aged woman wearing an old fashioned nurse's uniform standing next to the desk. "Here's a copy of a photograph we found when we were doing our preliminary research of Meadowlark. We believe it was taken in 1930 and it shows Mrs. Hightower, the head nurse standing in this very office. If you look to the left, you'll see the Victrola sitting on a table. For all you youngsters out there, it was the device on which phonograph records, called 78s back then were played. Mrs.

Hightower used to play the popular songs of the day, as well as classical music to soothe the patients. Since Vallee was such a huge star, I'm not surprised she's still playing his music almost a century later."

At the mention of Vallee's name, the music started up again. Levi eagerly recorded it while Sasha stood at his elbow, unable to believe what was happening.

"Mrs. Hightower, is that you still playing records for the patients?" Levi asked. "Are you here? Can you please confirm if it is you?" Suddenly the music stopped. "Don't stop!" Levi cried out. "If we somehow offended you, we're sorry. We really enjoyed the music. Please play it again."

Sasha surreptitiously rolled her eyes. Although it was exciting that they were actually hearing ghostly music, as far as she was concerned, the song was crap and the singer sounded like someone was dragging the lyrics through his nose.

You'd never make Number One today, that's for sure.

When she'd first brought up the idea of trying to get on TV with The Ghost Dudes, she hadn't really thought about whether she actually believed in the existence of ghosts. She considered them more as props to be used in horror novels or movies. Yet now, standing in a haunted building, hearing an honest-to-God two way communication between the living and the dead, she realized she was going to need to re-evaluate her assumptions about the possibility of life after death.

As Levi continued to urge Mrs. Hightower to play the music again, or speak into the recorder, she took the opportunity to flip through the pictures she'd taken on her digital camera. Pausing at each image, she grew increasingly disappointed that she hadn't captured anything. Come on! They'd just heard some crappy ghost song from the 1920's. She *had* to have captured something!

If there really are ghosts in this shithole, you better show up on my camera.

Just as she was nearing the last picture, she suddenly gasped. Quickly expanding the picture with her fingertips, she let out an exclamation.

"Holy crap! You guys are going to want to see this!"

***

Addison leaned against the wall in the hallway, her hand to her chest, trying her best to breathe despite the stuffy, dust filled air.

"Honey, are you alright?" Tina asked, her concerned face inches from Addison's.

She slowly nodded. "I—I'm sorry about that," she muttered.

"Hon, you had us scared to death when you fainted. Thank God you were only out a few moments. Are you sure you're okay?" Addison nodded again. "Can you tell us what you saw that made you scream and pass out?"

It was hard to speak with the camera practically in her face. She wanted nothing more than to push it away and get out of there as quickly as she could. Now she knew it had been a mistake to come here – a mistake to let Sasha talk her into this.

"Addison, can you describe what you saw? I'm sure the audience are dying to hear what you experienced."

Damn the audience! How can I tell them what I saw when the last thing I want to do is remember it?

Addison blinked back the helpless tears that stung her eyes. She couldn't break down in front of Tina and Reggie. And she certainly couldn't break down on television. She'd be the laughing stock of the world if she did that. She therefore took a deep breath and forced herself to calm down.

Don't think about it. Just say the words and get it over with.

"I saw a man standing in the corner of the room. He – he had his back to me. I don't know why, but I felt pulled towards him. Like I had to see who he was. He didn't move as I got closer. When I reached him and saw the agony on his face--" She felt her voice trembling, but she willed herself to go on. "He'd suffered so horribly. And the way he'd died –"

She couldn't continue as tears swelled in her throat.

"How did he die?" Tina asked quietly. "Take your time. This is important."

Addison wanted to scream into the camera. To beg the audience to leave her alone. But she couldn't. She'd signed a contract. She was on TV.

She was nothing but a performer. An actor on a stage. And this was her cue.

Still, her anger seeped into her words.

"He had a metal rod sticking out of his chest," she spat out. Then, despite her resolve not to, she began to cry. Tina quickly gathered her in her arms, gesturing to Reggie to make sure he'd gotten all of that on camera. He nodded.

"Reg, why don't you turn off the camera and give Addison a minute?"

She held the crying girl a few moments more, then gently disengaged herself.

"I'm so sorry you had to see that," she whispered.

"You didn't see anything?" Addison asked, raising her tear stained gaze to Tina. "Please tell me I'm not the only one who saw that."

"I knew there was someone in the room, but I was too concerned over you to focus," she responded. Before Addison could ask any more questions, she put her arm around the girl's shoulders and began to lead her down the corridor. "Why don't we go back to basecamp where you can chill? We still have a long night ahead of us and we're going to need you."

Addison stopped. "I'm not sure I can do any more. There's something here, Tina. Something evil. I think we're all in danger. The man I saw died in agony. What if what happened to him happens to one of us?"

Once again Tina gently pulled her along. "Addison, sometimes ghosts show us things to scare us off. They have their own secrets just like the living do, and they'll do whatever they can to make sure their secrets aren't revealed."

"Like kill us?" Addison asked.

Tina inwardly groaned. Damn, that had been the wrong thing to say. She didn't want to frighten the girl more than she already was. Hurrying to smooth over the situation, she said, "Ghosts don't kill. What they can do is scare you enough that you may end up hurting yourself. I guarantee you, you were shown that image to get you to react the way you're reacting now. Whatever is in here wants you to leave. It wants us all to leave." She noted the dubious look on Addison's face. "We had an investigation a few years back where I was literally tortured with nightmares before we even arrived. I got so scared I was ready to bag it and tell the guys to find another psychic to go with them. But I'm not a quitter and at the end of the day, I decided to go. It turned out the ghost haunting the house had committed a murder he'd never been arrested for. It didn't matter that he'd been dead for over a hundred years. He was determined to keep his secret, and he did everything he could to scare me so I wouldn't go and uncover what he'd done."

Her heart gave a leap when she saw Addison coming around.

"Wow, I never thought of ghosts being able to do that," the young girl whispered.

"Honey, you'd be surprised at how good they are at manipulating our emotions. So here's the plan. We'll take a break and grab something to eat before we start up again. How does that sound?"

Addison nodded wearily. She wasn't sure how she felt about Tina's words. They did make sense in a weird sort of way. This building probably had a gazillion secrets within its walls. Secrets that the patients and the staff probably didn't want revealed. But the man she'd seen had been so real. She'd felt his anguish, his pain. She didn't see him as trying to scare her.

She saw him as trying to warn her.

***

Sasha watched Devon's eyes widen in surprise as he looked at the photo. She also saw bewilderment before he quickly blinked it away.

Huh, that's weird. Instead of looking excited at what I got, he looks surprised.

"We'll need to run it through our computer. Not because of you, but because there are thousands of naysayers and skeptics out there just waiting to tear any and all evidence we gather apart. But from where I'm standing, I'd say you captured a real life ghost."

Ordinarily Sasha would have been dancing with joy. She'd captured something that wasn't easily captured. And she'd done it on live TV. However, the picture and Devon's behavior left her unsettled. He was acting like she shouldn't have captured anything at all. Which made no sense. Wasn't that why they were all here? To get something that proved ghosts were real? Was he jealous because she was the one who'd gotten it and not one of his own crew?

She again glanced down at the picture and inwardly shivered. Although she'd learned long ago never to show weakness of any kind, she had to admit – if only to herself – that the entire building was starting to leave her unsettled. There was something here that she couldn't quite put her finger on. An undercurrent that something wasn't right. It reminded her of the night six months earlier when she'd come home from visiting with Addison. As soon as she'd walked through the front door, she immediately knew something was wrong. She walked into the kitchen and found her mother sprawled out on the floor. She'd taken too much of her prescription medication and passed out. She'd come to just as Sasha was about to call for an ambulance.

It was that kind of feeling. A foreboding that things weren't what they seemed. Only deeper. And more frightening.

She could understand capturing a mist, or a shadow on film. She could even understand capturing the image of a woman dressed in a hospital gown since they were basically standing in a hospital that had once been filled with people dressed in hospital gowns.

What she couldn't understand was the sight of the apparition's face. A face contorted in a scream. A face with no eyes. Just two black holes staring back at the camera. Staring back at her.

She clicked off the photograph.

"Let's see if you got any EVPs," she said in an effort to push the image from her mind.

Levi rewound the recorder. He hit play as the small group gathered around him. They heard Levi speaking, asking the spirit to communicate. They even heard the sound of Devon moving behind the desk, and the soft clicking of Sasha's camera as she snapped away. They stared at each other in confusion.

They heard everything except the music.

"That's crazy," Devon said. "We all heard the song, right?" They all nodded. "Then why isn't it on the tape?"

No one had an explanation.

"I'm going to sing something, and I want you to tape it."

In a decidedly off-key timber, Devon attempted to sing Dancing with a Stranger by Sam Smith and Normani. When he was done, Levi played it back. Sasha cringed at his awful singing voice, but it was there on tape.

"Maybe the music was so low, we're not hearing it," Devon finally said. "I say we head back to basecamp and see if the computers picked up anything."

He jerked his head at Todd, who nodded. Turning, the cameraman led the group out of the room. "Come on guys. Follow me."

Devon waited until they were gone before scurrying back to the desk. He bent down and shoved his hand into one of the dark recesses beneath the desk. He took out the motion activated recorder and stared at it.

He'd placed the recorder there before the teenagers arrived, knowing it would provide a perfect dramatic moment in the show. In fact, he'd kept an eye on his phone that was showing the live broadcast and saw a spike in ratings when the music started playing. By moving behind the desk, he'd activated it on cue.

So why hadn't the music shown up on Levi's recorder?

He checked over the device and hit play. To his surprise, nothing happened. That was weird. He'd made sure to check it before placing it in the desk, and it had been working perfectly well.

Perplexed, he wondered if the batteries had somehow gone dead. They'd experienced batteries draining at some of their earlier investigations. Before the fame forced him to fake activity to keep the ratings going. Maybe Sasha really had captured a ghost that had somehow drained his recorder's batteries.

Turning the recorder over in his hand, he opened the panel and looked inside.

Devon cursed under his breath.

The batteries were gone.

Damn it, who had taken them? As far as he knew, after he'd planted the recorder, no one had come up here. And if one of the staff did wander upstairs, they'd have no reason to tamper with the recorder. They were just as invested in the success of this show as he was. Yet, as he pondered the mystery, a more important question slowly presented itself. A question that left him with an uneasy feeling in the pit of his stomach.

With the batteries removed from the recorder, what the hell did we hear?

***

As soon as Stan saw Addison enter basecamp, he forgot about manning the computers and hurried to her. Having seen most of what happened on the monitor, he was out of his mind with worry.

"Here," he said, handing her a bottle of water. "I also got you a sandwich. Hope you like ham and cheese."

She nodded and took a gulp of the water. "Did the camera capture what I saw?" she asked.

He shook his head. "But it doesn't mean you didn't see that ghost."

"I don't know what I saw."

"Yes you do, Addison. You know exactly what you saw."

While Stan tried to comfort the young woman, Tina sought out Mark and pulled him away from the group.

"Did you see that whole thing?" she asked.

"Yeah. It was really good. Between that girl's screams and Devon's set up of the music, our ratings went through the roof."

Tina shook her head. "Addison's a better actress than I ever imagined," she replied, an edge creeping into her voice. "She really had me going earlier when she found my pendant. I allowed myself to become convinced she's a powerful psychic. But a guy with a spike through his chest? That's too dramatic, even for me." Tina glanced in Addison's direction.

"She's a natural at heightening the fear and suspense. Jeez, I was about to faint myself when she went all zombie-like on me in the hallway."

Miffed that she'd been so easily taken in by Addison's innocent act, it took her a moment to realize Mark wasn't speaking. She glanced up at him and was surprised to see a look of fear on his face.

"What's the matter? You look weird."

"It's nothing."

"Bullshit it's nothing. We're a team, remember? Tell me what's wrong."

Mark pulled his hand through his dark hair. He hesitated, then let out his breath. He grabbed her arm and pulled her deeper into the shadows.

"Do you remember when Devon was telling the story of the German investigators?" he whispered.

She nodded. "Yeah. Six came in here, but only five emerged."

"Right. They never told anyone how their EVP specialist, Jurgen Knowles died."

"Uh huh. If I recall correctly, they just said he had an accident and left it at that." She glared at him. "What are you not telling me?"

"Devon managed to track down the team leader who finally admitted how Jurgen died. He's saving it for the big reveal."

Tina's heart began to beat rapidly. "You need to tell me, Mark. How did he die?" she forced herself to ask.

He raised his eyes until they met hers. "That girl was right in what she saw, Tee. She wasn't making it up."

CHAPTER SEVEN

"Out of respect for Jurgen's family, it was decided not to publicize the details of his death. The guy went up into the attic, even though they'd all been warned not to. He fell through the rotted floorboards. But when he landed, he didn't just land on the floor." Mark closed his eyes and took another deep breath. "They found him in the old chapel, on the altar. He'd been impaled on an iron rod that went right through his chest."

He watched the color drain from Tina's face. He'd worked on hundreds of investigations with her, and there'd been times where she'd appeared shaken. Overwhelmed. Distraught even. But he'd never seen her quite like this. Feeling suddenly guilty for *not* thinking his words through before blurting out how Jurgen had died, he reached out and patted Tina on the shoulder. "Hey. Are you okay? You're not looking too good."

Mark waited for Tina to respond. To say something. Anything, that would give him an indication that she wasn't about to faint. Or turn into a raving maniac. Finally, after several minutes, color returning, she said, "I told you this investigation was a mistake from the start. Can't you feel it? This place is vile. I don't give a crap about the ratings." Tina ran a shaky hand over her cheek. "Besides, what the hell will high ratings do if we're all dead!"

"Hold on, Tee." Mark grabbed Tina's upper arms and gave her a shake. In a harsh whisper, he said, "You need to keep your voice down. Do you hear yourself? You sound like a crazy woman."

On the verge of hysteria, she replied, "Seriously? Our lives may be in danger, and all you can think about is that I should keep my voice down? What, the crazy lady should play nice? Is that what you're telling me, Mark?"

Aware that he was only escalating matters, he tried a different approach. "Tina, take a breath before you blow a gasket." She glared at him. "Come on, Tee. Let's take a moment to be rational about this. You said yourself she was an amazing psychic. And as a psychic, she picked up on some dead guy. It happens. You of all people should know that."

As Mark spoke, an unexpected thought occurred to him. Maybe there was more to Tina's angst than the presumed evil that lurked at Meadowlark Asylum. In light of what he was thinking, her behavior suddenly made sense. Hell, he'd probably feel the same way if he was in her shoes. Voice thick with compassion, he said, "Tina, I think I know what's really going on here. You're our psychic, yet you didn't pick up on the ghost yourself. That's what has you so riled up."

Tina gasped. "Are you out of your mind? Is that why you think I'm upset?"

"Seems to me you didn't get so bent out of shape until you realized the kid was legit. Do you think just maybe, you might be a tiny bit jealous? I saw the video. You were okay with everything when you thought Addison might be a fraud. But now you're ticked off because you stood right beside her and didn't sense a thing. That's gotta sting." He shrugged. "Just sayin'."

Fists clenched by her side, Tina growled, "Why the hell are you not listening to me? I said it earlier and I'll say it again. How are you going to live with yourself if something happens to one of these kids?"

Mark felt his own temper rise. "If you're so scared, you can always grab one of the van keys and leave. No one is forcing you to stay."

Tina narrowed her eyes at him. "It seems I'm the only one who actually cares about these teenagers. Someone has to keep an eye on them and make sure they're safe, since you guys obviously won't." Turning on her heel, she stormed away.

Guilt washed over Mark. He tried to justify what he'd done by trying to convince himself it needed to be said. They all had healthy egos, but he couldn't allow Tina's emotions to cloud her judgment. He was only looking out for her best interests.

Wasn't he?

Mark's chest suddenly tightened at the path his thoughts took. He'd liked Tina from the first day they'd met. Probably way more than he should have. Unfortunately, his feelings had never been reciprocated, though maybe that was his fault. He didn't have a way with the ladies the way Devon did. His friend made it look so effortless, while he struggled and flopped about like a fish out of water. He'd come close so many times to telling her how much he cared, but he couldn't force the words out. He was terrified of being rejected. And now with the show consuming their lives, he couldn't risk having that kind of tension between them if she did end up telling him to take a hike.

So he swallowed his emotions and tried his best to concentrate on his career. Still, he felt unsettled by their conversation. Obviously, Tina was losing her objectivity where this investigation was concerned. And that wasn't good.

A pang of self-doubt washed over Mark as another thought occurred to him. Was he trying to convince himself that he was justified in his accusations? What if he'd misread Tina's intentions?

Needing a moment to think, Mark walked out into the foyer and sat down on the bottom step of the large set of stairs. He leaned forward and cupped his chin in his hand as he rested his elbow against his knee.

He'd certainly struck a nerve with Tina. He'd seen the hurt in her eyes before she stormed off. But that wasn't all that was troubling him. As much as he didn't want to admit it, what if Tina was right? The building was already getting to him. This investigation was different from all the ones they'd done before. He constantly felt as though he were being watched, even when he was alone. When he'd hopped out of the van and first stepped foot on this godforsaken property, he'd felt a sudden heaviness wash over him. A heaviness that continued to gnaw at him. Up until now he'd managed to convince himself it was nothing more than an over active imagination brought on by the knowledge of the horrors that took place on this nasty property. For a brief moment, he thought to speak with Devon about it. To see if he too was feeling it. But he instinctively knew it would be a waste of time. With all the pressure over getting the ratings up, and the spookiness of this place already producing results, Devon wasn't likely to listen to his concerns.

All I can do is keep my wits about me if I'm ever going to make it through this night.

Yet even as he thought this, he wondered if that was truly the best plan of action.

He inwardly cringed when he replayed in his mind's eye the video of Addison screaming and passing out. Except for Devon and himself, no one knew how Jurgen Knowles had really died. Yet Addison had pegged it. Why? Was Jurgen trying to tell them something?

Was he trying to warn her that she was in danger?

Was he trying to warn them all that they were in danger?

Tina was right about one thing. He couldn't live with himself if something happened to one of the teenagers. Or to one of their own crew. Reaching around, he unclipped the walkie-talkie from his waist belt.

Clicking the button, he said, "Devon. This is Mark. Do

you read me? Over."

After a few moments of static, Devon's voice erupted. "What's up, man? Everything okay?"

"Yeah. Hey, meet me in the entryway in five. We need to talk."

***

Devon scrambled into the foyer, Sasha, Levi and Todd, following close behind. "What's up, Dude? We've got a long night of investigating in front of us."

Mark glanced past Devon. With a furrowed brow, he said, "I need to talk to you in private."

With a look of frustration clearly evident on his face, Devon spun on his heel and addressed his team, "Sasha, Levi, why don't you go to basecamp and take five? I'll come get you when we're ready for Round Two of our investigation." After they'd gone, he turned to Todd. "Why don't you take a break as well? Don't go too far though. I've got some ideas I want to run by you."

Mark waited until he and Devon were alone before sharing what happened with Addison, as well as his conversation with Tina. His heart began to sink when he saw that the more he spoke, the grin on Devon's face grew wider. When he was done, Devon exclaimed, "Holy crap. That is outstanding!"

"Did you hear what I just said? That young girl actually collapsed on the floor. Maybe Tina has a point."

Devon grunted. "Tina is all about the drama. Take my advice, don't let her get into your head. As far as I'm concerned, she needs to get her act together, or she can take a walk. I'm good either way. As for Addison, I just saw her poking her head out of basecamp. She looked fine to me."

"Devon, she saw Jurgen! She saw him with the metal rod sticking out of his chest!"

"So what? It proves she's the real deal."

Mark rolled his eyes in frustration. "What if we're in over our heads here? What if this Monster of the Asylum isn't a legend? What if it really exists? What if it tries to hurt us?" He lowered his voice. "What if it tries to kill us?"

Devon chuckled as he faced his friend. "Mark, I've known you for over ten years. We've been through a lot of shit together. Do you honestly think I would put all of us in jeopardy?"

For the first time in all the years they'd been friends, Mark wondered if he really could trust Devon. He'd seen the changes in him since the show became popular. He lived, ate and breathed the show. Could he honestly believe Devon had their best interests at heart? Interests that might go against getting the all-important higher ratings?

Unfortunately, his passive nature took over. He hated confrontations and he knew what kind of reaction Devon would have if he stood his ground.

You're a coward, Mark. You just don't have the courage to stand up to him.

Hating himself for it, he shook his head. "I guess not," he muttered.

"Damn right, I wouldn't. Listen, I admit. This place is a lot more unsettling than I first expected. But it works to our advantage. I've been keeping an eye on the ratings. We've only been on the air for a few hours and they're already the highest we've ever had. We'd be insane to walk away from that."

Seeing the dejected look on his friend's face, Devon reached out and clasped his shoulder. "Tell you what. Why don't you and I go and check out the operating room for ourselves? We won't take Todd. We'll do our own investigation. It will look great to the audience at home that Devon and Mark are now going in alone where Addison had her terrifying experience. I'll grab the GoPro camera and let the others know." He started towards basecamp when he suddenly stopped. Turning back to Mark, he said, "So Tina didn't pick up on anything in the operating room?" Mark shook his head. "Interesting…" he murmured before disappearing into the room.

Mark didn't like the sound of that. In fact, he didn't like a lot of things. But he justified it by repeating to himself that it was all for the good of the show.

He started to follow Devon into the room to grab an EMF meter and recorder when he thought he heard a voice behind him. Thinking it was one of the teenagers or Tina, he spun around. There was no one there.

Puzzled, he wondered if it was the eeriness of the building that was starting to affect his senses. Yet, as he walked into basecamp, he couldn't rid himself of the feeling that he had heard a voice.

A voice that whispered, '*You fool*'.

***

After sending Levi, Tina and Reggie out to the third floor, and leaving Addison and Sasha to chill out a bit longer, Mark and Devon retraced the path Tina and Addison had taken not more than a half hour before.

Chunks of old plaster and bits of shattered glass from broken wall lanterns crackled and snapped beneath their boots, echoing loudly down the barren and ill-kempt hallway. Devon let out a low whistle. "On the creep factor scale of one to ten, I'd say this place ranks up there at an eleven. Definitely worth every penny the network had to spend to get the town to open it up again."

"You honestly don't feel anything in here?"

"Not anything to speak of. Okay, I have noticed a couple of odd things since we got here. But nothing that can't be explained away. Come on, you and I both know that the dead can't hurt the living." At least he hoped not. Right now, he still didn't know what to make of his investigation with Sasha and Levi. The music that, by all rights, shouldn't have been playing. Not from a recorder with no batteries. Nor the fact that it wasn't captured by the recorder.

What the hell was that all about? Who was behind it? And what game were they playing?

His suspicions automatically centered on Tina. With every investigation, she was becoming more of a pain in the ass diva, with her demands and ridiculous ideas that she could actually run this team. *His* team. He wouldn't put it past her to pull something like this to discredit him. God, it was so satisfying to hear Mark tell him she hadn't picked up anything in the room with Addison. That really had to be getting her shorts in a twist. She'd actually been upstaged on live TV. By a sixteen year old teenager. Woo-hoo, talk about karma! As of yet, he didn't have any proof that she'd stolen the batteries from the recorder. But he'd keep an eye on her. Sooner or later, she'd slip up. And when she did, he'd fire her ass and finally get the bitch out of his life once and for all.

"Are you so sure the dead can't hurt the living?"

Mark's question pulled Devon out of his thoughts. "With all of the investigations we've done, I think we'd know by now. Ghosts are intangible. Nonphysical energy. Jeez, man," Devon laughed. "Stop being a big baby. God, I thought Tina was the drama queen on the team."

"Did you ever stop to consider that sometimes she could be right?" Devon guffawed. "Look what's already happened with Addison. We're responsible for these kids, Devon. And this place is *not* like any other investigation we've done."

"So what you saying? You want to end this now? Pack up our things and tell the network and the audience that we're bailing because Addison fell down and went boom? Seriously? Is that what you're suggesting?"

He turned and faced Mark, his face mottled with anger in the glow of the flashlight.

A thousand emotions ran through Mark. At the end, however, he simply said, "I'm suggesting we be more alert, that's all."

"That I can do."

They walked a few feet further before Mark stopped before a door. "This is the operating room," he announced. He grabbed the door handle only to yelp out in pain as he jerked his hand back. "Holy shit! The handle is burning up!" he exclaimed as he cradled his hand against his chest.

"Don't be ridiculous," Devon scoffed. "The temperature in this place can't be more than fifty degrees, and without heat, it's getting colder by the minute."

"Then how do you explain this?"

Mark held his hand out. Devon raised his flashlight and frowned when he saw the unmistakable burn marks on his palm and fingers.

Before he could respond, a frightening thought occurred to him. Mark had never questioned his motives or intentions before. Yet here he was, ready to walk away from an investigation that was their only chance at holding onto their fame. Their careers.

Was Tina behind all of this?

He knew how Mark felt about her. A blind man could see the look on his face whenever Tina walked into the room. Was he allowing his feelings for her to lure him into conspiring against his best friend? His chest tightened at the thought that he couldn't trust Mark anymore.

Reaching a decision to play along until he could figure out just what was going on, he said, "Move aside, I'll open the door." Pushing away his hesitation, he grabbed the handle. It was cool to the touch. He threw a curious look at Mark, who responded with bewilderment. *Was this part of their plan? Were they trying to set him up for a fall?*

"I don't understand," Mark stammered. "The door handle was hot. You saw the burn marks!" He held out his hand again, the red skin still showing.

"Well, it's not hot now. Obviously," Devon added sarcastically.

The rusted hinges squealed as he shoved the door open and stepped inside. He turned around to see his friend standing at the threshold. "Are you coming in?"

Still baffled over what had just happened, Mark gingerly stepped through and joined him.

Standing in the center of the room, Devon raised the flashlight, slowly scanning from left to right. "Where exactly was Addison standing when she collapsed?"

"Over there," Mark pointed to the far right. They started towards the area when Devon's flashlight reflected against something shiny. "Wow, will you look at that! It's an old operating table. That is beyond freaky."

A loud, guttural scream ripped through the silence.

Struggling to balance the flashlight he held in one hand and the EMF meter in the other, Devon attempted to cover his ears against the shattering screeching that continued to bombard him. He turned to Mark to gauge his reaction and was shocked to see his friend staring back at him in confusion. "Don't you hear that?" he shouted over the incessant screams that seemed to be coming at him from all sides.

"Hear what?"

Devon gritted his teeth as he realized he'd just been had. A moment later, the screaming abruptly stopped. He turned his fury on Mark.

"I don't know what kind of game you and Tina are playing, but I swear, if you sabotage this investigation, I'm suing the both of you."

Mark took a step back, his brow furrowed with worry. "Whatever it was you just heard, it *was not me*. Or Tina. We keep trying to tell you, this place is evil. We're in over our heads, Devon. It's trying to pit us against each other, and it appears to be succeeding."

"You're full of shit, Mark. You and that bitch are not going to win this."

Sighing with frustration, Mark threw his hands up in the air. "You just won't listen, will you? I'm done, Devon."

Turning on his heel, he stomped out of the room.

Finding himself alone, it took a few moments for Devon to regain his composure, although he still grappled with the hurt of Mark's betrayal. After all they'd been through, he couldn't believe Mark was now stabbing him in the back. However, now was not the time to worry about it. He'd worry about it when the show was over.

Determined to refocus on the investigation, Devon suddenly became aware of the sound of dripping, followed by the incessant droning of insects buzzing. Huh? That wasn't here before.

He snapped the flashlight in the direction of the sound.

He jumped when the EMF meter suddenly began to blare, piercing his ear drums. Quickly turning it off, he swung the beam of light around the room. He frowned when he noticed the operating table. Hadn't it been closer just moments ago? Now it was standing on the other side of the room. How was that possible? Surely he would have heard it moving.

As he struggled to make sense of it all, he suddenly realized it was another one of Tina and Mark's hoaxes. That's why Mark had stormed off. He wanted to make sure Devon was alone so he'd be more prone to being spooked.

Damn it. He couldn't believe how determined they were to bring him down. His first impulse was to leave, and not give them the satisfaction of drawing him into their plot. Yet, he had to admit, he was curious to see exactly what they'd set up. Or whether it was a trick he could use himself in the future.

The dripping and buzzing grew louder, prompting him to move closer in the direction of where the sound was coming from. To his surprise, he realized the sounds were coming from the old operating table. Determined to find out how the hoax had been engineered, he took a step closer. Suddenly, the smell of rotting meat seared his nostrils, causing him to physically gag.

What kind of crap are they trying to pull off here?

Clasping his hand over his mouth and nose to mask the nauseating smell, he once again considered leaving the room. Yet he couldn't or wouldn't show any weakness.

I wouldn't put it past Tina to set up a live camera feed in the room to try and humiliate me.

With this thought in mind he approached the table and shone his flashlight downwards. He swallowed a scream as a decaying corpse of a male patient looked back at him. Lying on the table, bloated with death, body fluid dripping onto the floor Devon saw a trail of maggots squirming over what was left of the corpse's face.

Unable to turn away, and determined to prove it a hoax, Devon reached out with his finger and poked at what he believed was a holographic image. To his horror, he felt his finger sink into an ice-cold, jelly-like substance that had once been skin.

Crying out in shock and fear, he stumbled back so quickly, he fell to the floor.

The flashlight flew out of his hand and crashed against the wall, plunging him into darkness. Terrified that he was now alone in a dark room, with a rotting corpse, Devon jumped to his feet and felt around for the flashlight. Finally, he felt the cold metal and grasped it in his hands.

With his heart pounding in his chest, Devon flicked the flashlight on, and aimed it back towards the body. Gasping aloud, he hurried to the table and inspected all around it, but there was nothing there.

The body had disappeared.

CHAPTER EIGHT

"Okay, we have Levi, Tina and Reggie investigating the administrator's office," Brandon announced to the group gathered at basecamp. "Has anyone seen Devon? He's not showing up on any of the camera feeds and he's not responding to the walkie-talkie."

"I left him up in the operating room," Mark replied.

"Why didn't he come back with you?"

He shrugged, not willing to reveal the argument the two had.

Brandon shook his head in disgust. "I hate when he goes off on his own. He should know better by now." He lifted his gaze and looked at the group. "I need another team to go out so we can switch back and forth between Tina's group and whoever goes out. We have to keep it interesting for the folks watching at home." He looked at each of the teenagers, then pointed at Sasha and Addison. "You two haven't gone out together yet. I think the audience would enjoy watching you two investigate. Since Tina, Levi and Reggie are on the third floor, why don't you go up to the second floor? There's a recreation room near the center of the building that supposedly has a lot of activity. Todd, you'll continue to act as cameraman for them."

"What about Devon?" Addison asked. "I don't like the fact that he's alone in this building."

"I'll try to raise him again on the walkie-talkie. I'm sure he's setting up—" Brandon caught himself. He glanced at the teenagers before adding, "I'm sure he's setting up some shots in his head. You know what a perfectionist he is."

"Are you up to it?" Stan asked Addison in a low whisper. She hesitated for a moment before nodding.

"The show must go on," she replied grimly.

"I'll keep an eye on you and Sasha the whole time on the monitor. Any sign of trouble, you get the hell out of there ASAP."

She nodded and together with Sasha and Todd, the three left the room.

"I'm going to go outside and get a breath of fresh air," Mark announced abruptly. Before Brandon could respond, he turned and left.

"I'm not sure about this," Stan said as he sat back down in front of the monitors. "Addison seems unsteady."

"I understand that, which is why I had Todd go with them. He's more compassionate than Reggie. I'm sure he'll keep an eye on her. Besides," he added, with a mischievous gleam in his eye. "Whenever Addison is on screen, the ratings spike. She's a natural. We can't take her off the air now."

"Yeah, but I'm worried about her."

He gave Stan a knowing smile. "She is very sweet, isn't she?" Stan blushed. "Don't worry, bro. She'll be fine. You should have seen us during our first television investigation. We didn't know our ass from our elbow. It was a bit of a disaster. But we got better at it. You guys will too."

Stan turned his attention back to the monitor that was fixed on Addison and her group.

Although he didn't have a psychic bone in his body, Stan was beginning to feel the weird vibe in the building. And as much as he disliked Devon Watson, he couldn't help worrying where the man had gone to.

"Are you sure Devon is okay?" he asked Brandon, who was seated next to him and also watching the monitors. "He's been gone a long time."

Brandon turned an eye towards the young man. "Kid, in case you haven't noticed, Devon likes to be the star attraction. I guarantee you, he's somewhere in this mausoleum trying his best to figure out how to look great on camera."

"But should he be alone? I mean, after what happened to Addison…"

"If there's anyone who knows how to take care of himself, it's Devon. You wouldn't know it by looking at him, but he grew up in one of Chicago's toughest neighborhoods. That's why this show means so much to him. Actually, it's why it means so much to all of us. We were nobodies until The Ghost Dudes hit it big. None of us are exactly anxious to slide back into obscurity any time soon."

"But what if there really is something malicious in here?" Stan persisted. "What if we're all just sitting ducks?"

Brandon clapped his hand on Stan's back. "We were investigating for a couple of years before we got the TV show. This place is no different than dozens of other places we've checked out, not only here, but in Europe as well. Don't worry, we know what we're doing."

Stan didn't believe him, but he had nothing to offer as proof to how he was feeling. He had no choice but to turn his attention back to the screen. Devon and his gang may not care about the potential for danger in this building, but he did. And he'd be damned if he allowed anything to happen to his friends. He therefore kept a sharp eye on the screens showing Addison and her team, and Levi and Tina. If he saw even a hint of anything that might be dangerous, he'd call it out and run to help.

He only hoped he'd get there in time.

***

"Can you imagine spending the rest of your days holed up in this sad room with nothing to do but play checkers and gin rummy?" Sasha asked as she, Addison and Todd entered the long, rectangular room that had once served as a recreational gathering place for the more manageable patients.

As their shoes crunched over broken glass and plaster, they saw the remains of what had passed for recreation. Playing cards were strewn around the room, Chinese checker and other board games were lying about haphazardly, as though someone had gathered them in their arms and thrown them up into the air, leaving them where they fell.

"It feels so depressing in here," Addison said as she slowly walked around, closely followed by Todd who was capturing everything on camera.

"Are you picking up on anyone in particular?" Sasha asked as she clicked off photographs.

"Yeah, take your time and see what you get," Todd added.

Addison remained silent as she continued moving around the room. She felt as though she'd been thrown into the deep end of a pool without a life preserver. They were looking to her to be the psychic, to make otherworldly announcements. God, she felt like such a fake. The episode with the shadow had been a fluke. That's all. A weird fluke. She was no more psychic than Sasha or Levi or even Stan with his computer-like brain.

Is this what Aunt Juliette feels like when people show up at her house, expecting her to give them all the answers they won't find for themselves?

The camera following her every step felt like a ten-ton weight hanging over her.

Get a grip. Your friends are counting on you to not make idiots of them and of yourself. Do something! Anything!

Addison stopped and closed her eyes, taking a deep breath to center herself. She suddenly felt overcome by what felt like a whirlwind of energy, coming at her from all sides.

"Wow, that's crazy," she blurted out.

"What's crazy?" Sasha asked.

"There's a lot of energy coming in. It's all over the place. I can't seem to get a handle on it."

"Makes sense. This was a place where people gathered," Todd answered. "And considering the mental state they were in…"

Addison cringed. Of course there would be all sorts of energy in a room like this. Could she be more obvious?

Feeling like a complete idiot, Addison turned away from the camera and continued moving about the room. As she glanced about at the sad reminders of the people who had once inhabited these walls, she remembered something Aunt Juliette had once told her.

Our thoughts and emotions are very strong. Much stronger than we even realize. Wherever humans go, we leave traces of that energy. That's how sensitive people like you and me know when there's been an argument in a room, even if the people who were arguing have gone. We feel the energy that was left behind. Now take that one step further. Think about an area where something traumatic has happened. It actually leaves a scar in time. Anyone who is even the slightest bit sensitive will feel it. They may not understand what it is, but it doesn't mean that what they're feeling doesn't exist.

Addison could only guess at the kinds of trauma suffered here. But if Aunt Juliette was right, the whirling, indecipherable energy she felt had to have been left behind by the poor forgotten souls who'd once walked these halls, and sat in this room.

She spied a chess piece lying on the floor. Bending down to pick it up, her fingers touched the dusty wooden carving of a knight.

"Violence. Lots of violence," she whispered under her breath.

She was shocked at what she said. But she couldn't stop herself. It was as if she were sitting in the back of her own brain and watching herself speak words that weren't hers, but that she had no control over.

"So much violence. And anger. They want desperately to escape. They can't." Addison lifted her head and stared at the doorway they'd just entered through. "But they will," she murmured. "In spite of him, they will."

The chess piece slipped out of her fingers and fell to the floor. The jarring sound pulled Addison out of her trance-like state and she shook her head as if to clear it. She looked up and was shocked to see both Sasha and Todd staring at her.

"What?" she asked, defensively.

"Who's he?" Sasha questioned.

"I don't know what you're talking about."

"Addison, do you not know what you just said?"

Fear gripped the young woman. What had she done? Had she made an ass out of herself? Again?

"I had Sasha tape it on her phone," Todd spoke up. "Play it for her, Sash."

She gave Addison her phone and hit play. The teenager watched in mounting horror and embarrassment as the image of herself showed someone she didn't even know. Her face looked strange. Blank. And her green eyes looked almost black as she looked across the room and said the strange words about 'him'. Who the hell was 'him'? What was she talking about?

Terrified that she'd so easily lost control, she handed back the phone with shaking fingers.

"I –" She started, only to have the words dry up in her throat.

Sensing her discomfort, Sasha shoved the phone in her back pocket. She then turned to Todd.

"Okay dude, I think it's about time you came clean. What exactly happened here at Meadowlark Asylum?

***

Devon was angry. All the way back to basecamp, he'd racked his brains trying to figure out how the stunt had been pulled off. It reinforced his suspicions that Mark and Tina were in cahoots to sabotage, not only this investigation, but his entire career. Why though? Because she actually believed she was psychic? Was he supposed to drop everything and bow down to her every time she got a *feeling?* Hell would freeze over before he ever allowed that to happen. Yet even as his temper boiled, he wondered how they'd been able to pull something this elaborate off. Mark wasn't a stupid man, but he wasn't a technical genius either. Neither was Tina.

Although he'd never admit it, he'd almost had a heart attack when he'd seen that disgusting corpse on the table. And he'd almost thrown up when he'd watched the revolting maggots crawling around its face. And don't even get him started on the nauseating smell, or the feel of the rotted flesh against his fingertip. Yet it had all abruptly disappeared when he fell on the floor.

There was only person who could set up something like that. Someone who had the technical and imaginative skills. Although the stunt had been spectacular, it wasn't something Mark or Tina or even Devon would ever have dreamed up. His heart sank as his temper reignited.

Is everyone turning against me?

He rounded the corner and walked into basecamp where he found Brandon and the other little dweeb sitting in front of the monitors.

"The conquering hero finally returns," Brandon smiled sarcastically, turning at the sound of Devon's steps.

"We were worried about you," Stan said. "Where did you go?"

"Scoping out some other areas I thought we could investigate," he answered. Turning to Brandon, he said curtly, "I need to talk to you in private."

He turned on his heel and went into the hallway. Brandon looked at Stan and shrugged.

"Gotta go feed the ego," he quipped before he got up and followed Devon into the dark and gloomy foyer.

"I'm beginning to think fame is not worth the hassle," Stan said aloud to himself before turning his attention back to the monitors. He'd seen Addison go into a strange kind of trance-like state. Thank God it had only lasted a few moments. But he wasn't taking any chances. He leaned over and peered at the screen.

***

"Why didn't you tell me?"

Brandon stared at Devon in bewilderment. "What are you talking about, dude?"

"You know very well what I'm talking about. Don't you ever pull something like that again without consulting me first, or your ass is fired."

"Since when do you decide who gets fired?" Brandon shot back.

"It's my group. I started it."

"Bullshit. *We* started it. You, Mark and me."

"Did Tina put you up to this?"

Brandon shook his head in frustration. "I honestly have no idea what you're talking about. And where the hell have you been for the last half hour? Mark returned to basecamp, but you didn't. You know the rules. You don't take off without letting one of us know where you're going. And I don't appreciate you ignoring me on the walkie-talkie either."

Devon narrowed his eyes. "You're shitting me, right? You set everything up, including putting a camera in the operating room, yet you *didn't* get it on film?"

"Read my lips, bro. I don't have a clue what you're talking about. I haven't seen you on screen since you and Mark took off to have your private little investigation. Which, by the way, was a total waste of time since you never filmed any of it."

"Where's Mark now?"

"He stepped outside to get some air."

Devon glared at Brandon. As much as he hated to admit it, he felt the technician was telling the truth. He took a deep breath and let it out slowly.

"Some weird shit is going on," he seethed. "We need to review the tapes."

He started to brush past Brandon when he felt himself pulled back.

"The kid's in there."

"Damn, that's right."

"Don't worry," Brandon said. "I'll take care of it."

They returned to basecamp and Brandon slid back into his seat.

"Hey Stan, we're getting reports that one of the motion sensor cameras is down up on the third floor near the cafeteria. Go check it out, will you?"

Stan turned a dubious eye towards him. "You want me to go up there? *Alone?*"

"Being a paranormal investigator is all about facing your fears," Devon barked. He softened his tone as he quickly added, "You'll be on camera the whole time. And I think Tina and her crew are up in that area anyway. You'll be fine."

Unable to refuse, Stan reluctantly got up and grabbed a flashlight and a small case of tools from a nearby table. He threw the two one last look before heaving himself out of the room.

Once he was gone, Devon leaned over Brandon. "Bring up the tape where that young psychic passes out. What's her name – Annie, Angela."

"Addison," Brandon corrected him as he quickly pulled up the tape. The two watched silently as the event replayed itself.

"Now switch over to when we were in the head nurse's office."

"Yeah, what happened there? That was guaranteed to be brilliant. I thought you had the recorder set up."

"That's the thing. I did. And we heard Rudy Vallee singing."

Brandon swung around in his chair and stared at Devon. "That's impossible. I didn't hear a thing. Something must have gone wrong with Todd's audio."

"His audio was fine. So was Levi's recorder. But neither picked up the music, even though we heard it."

"That's insane."

"Tell me about it." Devon then shared with Brandon the image Sasha had captured on her camera, as well as what he'd experienced in the operating room with the decaying corpse. Brandon's eyes widened in shock.

"No wonder you went apeshit if you think one of us set that up."

"If it wasn't you, then it had to be Tina and Mark."

The technician shook his head. "They don't have that kind of knowledge or expertise." He paused, then threw his friend a side glance. "Devon, have you considered the alternative? Instead of going off half-cocked blaming Tina and Mark, maybe you actually had some kind of paranormal experience."

Devon snorted. "Oh please."

"How else can you explain what you went through? Okay, Addison could have been acting. No one saw what she saw. But you're saying you all heard the music, yet it wasn't picked up by either the camera, or the recorder. And when you checked, the batteries were gone. Then you're telling me you saw a rotting corpse that suddenly disappeared. If that isn't paranormal, then I don't know what is."

He frowned when he saw the dark look on Devon's face. "Why are your shorts in a knot? This is fantastic, bro! You actually had an encounter with the Other Side. I think you ought to go on camera and explain what just happened. That will get the viewers at home all excited. I'll play back the scene in the operating room where Addison screams and faints. I guarantee you people will be calling in thinking they saw something. Happens all the time. The power of suggestion is a wonderful thing."

"Okay, let's shoot it."

While Brandon went to grab a camera, Devon positioned himself against the far wall. By all rights, he should be excited. Brandon was right. This was going to send the ratings spiking. Yet he couldn't rid himself of a disquiet that ate away at him.

He was accustomed to always being in control. In every investigation they'd ever done, even before the TV gig came along, he was the one who oversaw everything. He made sure the level of suspense and fear was evenly spaced, keeping what he considered a rhythm to their work.

But what he was going through in this building was new. He felt himself losing control of the investigation. And he didn't like it. Mark's words suddenly threw themselves at him.

Maybe we're in over our heads.

No! he shouted back in his mind's eye. We are *not* over our heads. And I am *not* losing control. This is just a dilapidated old building that should have been torn down years ago. The only ghosts in here are the ones in our imaginations.

He calmed himself with the thought of the other tricks he'd rigged up that he'd debut throughout the night. They promised to be spectacular and put them back at number one.

"Are you ready?" Brandon asked as he stood in front of Devon with the camera aimed towards him.

"Yes, I am."

"Okay. In three, two, one."

The red light on the camera came on and Devon smiled. "Wait until you hear what happened to me upstairs. You're not going to believe it."

CHAPTER NINE

Todd calmly met Sasha's angry eye. "I know as much about this place as you do."

"That's crap and you know it," she snorted. "You've been working with these guys for what? Two years? Ever since the show went on the air? You honestly expect me to believe that you aren't part of any discussions that talk about the places you investigate?"

He shrugged. "That's right. I'm not a member of The Ghost Dudes. I'm just the cameraman. They tell me where to point the lens and I do it. That's what I was hired for."

"Let it go, Sash," Addison replied wearily. "It's not that important."

Sasha swung around and faced her friend. "Not important? You just took a trip to the Twilight Zone and you don't think that's important?"

Addison held her hand up. She was surprised to find how heavy her arm felt. It must be the building. It was draining her. Although she appreciated Sasha's loyalty, the Latina's anger was also sapping her energy.

"There's no reason for Todd to lie. The person who holds all the cards is Devon. Let's just get on with it. The sooner we finish this investigation, the sooner we can get out of here."

And that couldn't come fast enough.

***

Mark sat on the stone steps leading into the asylum. The

night was silent, and the woods surrounding the building looked especially dark and frightening. Once again he had the uncomfortable feeling that he was being watched. He'd given up smoking several years before, but right now he'd give anything to have a cigarette, if only to calm him down. Before he could stop himself, the argument replayed itself in his mind's eye.

Devon's behavior was over the top. Mark had no explanation for it, unless it was, as he suspected, the building affecting all their moods. He thought back to Tina's warnings about the malevolence stalking the hallways. The more he experienced, the more he realized she was right.

Why wouldn't Devon see that?

Why was he so hellbent on finishing this investigation in a building that didn't want them there? And was doing all it could to set them against each other?

He took a deep breath and let it out slowly, watching it vaporize in the cold night air before disappearing.

He glanced at the row of vans parked in front of the steps. If he was smart, he'd go inside, grab a set of keys and drive as far away from here as he possibly could.

I can't abandon Tina. And as much as he's a complete asshole, I can't abandon Devon here either. Or Brandon. Or anyone, for that matter.

Reluctantly concluding that he had no choice but to go back inside, he took one last deep breath and stood up. Climbing up the steps, he grabbed the door handle and pulled it towards him. To his surprise, the door wouldn't open.

"Are you kidding me?" he asked aloud as he tried several times to pull it open. How was that possible? The door could only be locked from the outside, and only with a key. So why wouldn't it open?

He banged on it several times and called out, but no one responded. Just as he was reaching for his walkie-talkie to alert the others of his predicament, the hairs suddenly stood up on the back of his neck. Forcing himself to turn his head, he gazed back at the woods. An overwhelming sense of being watched flooded his senses. There was something out there. Observing him. Waiting.

He had a stark moment of clarity when a thought crashed into his consciousness.

I have to get back into this building or I won't see the morning.

Close to panic, Mark started to grab his walkie-talkie. Without warning, the wind suddenly came up with a force that physically pushed him against the door. He threw his hands up to protect his face as leaves and grit pummeled him.

"Help! Help!" he screamed. He tried the door again, but it refused to budge.

Frantic with fear, it took Mark a moment to realize he was hearing moaning within the sharp gusts of air.

"For God's sake, let me in! Please!" he pleaded above the roar of the wind.

To his astonishment, the wind intensified its ferocity. He felt a chill run down his spine when he heard what sounded like laughter interspersed with each gust. He tried to stand, to make a run for it. But he couldn't move. The wind had him pinned against the door.

He was helpless.

And at the mercy of whatever was in the woods.

Suddenly, Mark felt himself fall backwards as the door abruptly opened. Before he knew what was happening, he felt the front of his jacket grabbed and he was jerked back from toppling down the stairs.

Devon stared at Mark's disheveled appearance. His hair was standing on end and his jacket was covered in bits of dead leaves and dirt.

"What's the matter with you?" Devon asked. "You look like hell."

Mark stared at him wordlessly before pushing past him and

entering the building.

***

Thankfully, at least to Stan's mind, the rest of the investigations went smoothly. After hearing Sasha's exchange with Todd, they were now walking along the corridor. He was concerned over the exhaustion plainly evident on Addison's face, but so far, she appeared to be keeping up with the others.

Glancing at the other monitor, he watched as Tina, Levi and Mark, who had unexpectedly joined them five minutes before, made their way through what had once been the cafeteria. It was dark and filled with spider webs, but that too was quiet. There was the occasional sound of what Tina insisted was someone moaning, but when it was played back on camera, Stan heard nothing. He did think Mark looked a little off, as if his mind wasn't on the investigation, but who was he to question it?

He sat back in his chair with a sigh. By now, he was completely bored. He'd been sitting there for four hours and, with the exception of Addison blanking out twice, nothing else had happened that was worth getting excited about. He couldn't understand how The Ghost Dudes could do this week after week. He'd go stark raving mad if he had to sit at a monitor and watch his friends walk up and down the corridors for hours, thinking they heard something, only to find out it was probably an old house settling. Or gas.

He sipped on a coke, hoping the caffeine would keep him from falling asleep. He glanced at Brandon every once in a while, and usually found him gaming on his phone.

So much for watching your friends' back.

He was supposed to be manning the texts pouring in from the audience, but he'd asked Stan to do it. It wasn't long before Stan realized why he'd shifted the responsibility onto his shoulders. Between keeping a sharp eye on Addison, he occasionally glanced at the messages.

And rolled his eyes.

Jeez, people were actually saying they'd seen a huge reptilian like creature standing behind Addison that could only be the Monster of the Asylum, while others swore they'd seen the image of a young boy laughing at Tina and Mark. A few others were convinced they'd seen a black dog which started an online argument over which was truly the Monster of the Asylum.

Stan found it all ridiculous. He'd been staring at the monitors for hours and had seen none of those things.

Either these people are crazy, or they're allowing their imaginations to go into overdrive.

Turning away from the texts that seemed endless, he focused on the image of Devon flickering on the top right hand monitor. Although he'd promised no one would be investigating alone, there he was, poking around several of the abandoned patients' rooms with just the GoPro camera and an EVP meter to keep him company. Stan wondered if Devon's decision to go solo had anything to do with the odd conversation he'd overheard between Devon and Brandon when he'd returned from checking on the motion detector that went off as soon as he walked in front of it.

Broken, my ass. Those two wanted me out of basecamp, though I can't figure out why yet.

"How are things going?" Devon had asked as he stood over Brandon.

"Honestly, after what happened to Addison, it's slowed down. A lot," Brandon answered. The two exchanged glances.

"I've got it covered," Devon responded. "I'll head up to the second floor and see if I can provoke any spirits. I usually get a response when I call them out."

Although the exchange sounded innocent at first, the more Stan thought about it, the more it felt off. He slid into his chair and waited until Devon was gone.

"I hate when Devon does that. It sounds so disrespectful when he yells and screams at them," he said.

"It gets results," Brandon answered.

"Yeah, but who are we to judge? These were living and breathing people once. We don't know what their lives were like. We don't know what made them what they were. Do we honestly have the right to yell and insult and criticize them?"

Brandon turned and blinked at the teenager. "If you're looking to philosophize about loving your fellow man and forgiving their sins and understanding an individual's soul journey, you've come to the wrong place."

It was not what Stan had expected to hear. As Brandon turned back to his gaming, Stan reluctantly shifted his gaze to Devon.

So much for trying to bring in a little compassion.

He watched as Devon entered yet another patient room. There was a chair sitting near the window, and a bed frame leaning upright against one of the walls.

Despite his suspicions about Devon, he had to hand it to the guy. He'd hated going upstairs alone. He'd dashed up as quickly as he could, looked at the sensor and run back downstairs. He knew he didn't have the guts to walk around this place alone. He wasn't sure he had to guts to walk around this place with the high school football team surrounding him.

"I'm here on the second floor in another patient room," Devon intoned into the camera microphone. "As you can imagine, the place is full of dust and broken plaster on the floor. I need to be careful I don't trip and fall." The camera panned the room slowly.

"The asylum was built in 1869 and it's hard to imagine all the people who once called this room home. The medical establishment didn't have the understanding of mental illness we do today. In those days, you could be thrown into a place like this for having a child out of wedlock. Or being overly emotional. Hard to imagine, but it's true."

Stan observed as Devon slowly made his way around the small room. The guy was obviously a professional. He spun a story that was interesting and was surely keeping the audience's attention. He glanced at the messages and saw how right he was. The argument over whether the Monster of the Asylum was a tall reptilian or a black dog had now morphed into an argument over health care in the 19th century.

As Devon listed the different reasons people could be committed to a mental asylum over a century before, he was suddenly interrupted when the chair that had been sitting near the window visibly moved at least two inches across the floor.

"Wow!" Stan exclaimed as he jumped back in his chair.

Brandon looked up as Devon hurriedly explained what had just happened.

"We'll play back the tape so you can see what I just saw," he said.

Brandon hit a button and the tape was replayed where the chair was plainly seen to move.

"That's incredible!" Devon cried out. "I'm going to take my recorder out and see if we can find out who did that."

While Devon fiddled with the recorder, Brandon played the tape yet again. Stan watched it for the third time. He leaned forward and just as the tape ended, he gasped.

"Amazing stuff, huh?" Brandon said as he saw the shocked look on Stan's face. "I love it when the ghosts decide to cooperate."

Stan nodded as he continued to watch Devon go through an EVP session. He waited until the man wrapped up the investigation and left the room before standing up.

"I need to go to the bathroom. I'll be right back."

"Don't forget, the porta potty is right outside the front door."

"Thanks."

Stan grabbed a flashlight and walked out of basecamp. Instead of heading outside though, he turned right and ran up the stairs. He hated the thought of roaming around this place alone again, but he needed to check the veracity of what he'd just seen. He promised himself to get it over with as quickly as possible and dash back to basecamp before the reptilian, or the dog, or whatever the Monster was even knew he was up here.

He hoped.

Coming out onto the second floor landing, he had just enough time to duck into a room before Devon passed by and headed down the stairs. Hearing his footsteps fade away, Stan scurried down the hallway until he reached the room that looked like the one Devon had just vacated.

Sneaking inside, he knew he had to move the camera so Brandon wouldn't see what he was up to. Crawling along the dusty floor, just out of view of the lens, he made sure not to get any broken glass or sharp pieces of tile imbedded in his palms. Reaching the camera, he lifted his hand and grabbed the swivel where the tripod and camera met. Holding his breath, he very slowly moved the camera until it was pointing at the wall behind it.

Confident he couldn't be seen, Stan stood up and tried to wipe the dust and grime from his jeans. He then approached the chair. Holding his flashlight in his mouth, he ran his hands along the seat and the spindles. Almost immediately, his fingers came up against what felt like a wire. Taking his flashlight out of his mouth, he shone it down and traced the razor thin cable from the chair right to the spot where Devon had been standing when the chair moved. All he'd needed to do was move the wire with his leg to make the chair jerk forward.

"Damn," he whispered under his breath.

Nearly invisible to the human eye, he'd only seen it because of a slight reflection in the camera light when the chair moved. With the audience fixated on the chair itself, he doubted anyone else had seen it.

But he had.

And it made him angry.

"They really are fakes," he whispered aloud to himself. "This whole show is nothing but lies and deception."

Caught up in his disappointment and outrage, he didn't at first feel the abrupt drop in temperature. When he shivered and the hairs on his arms and on the back of his neck stood up, Stan suddenly realized he wasn't alone.

Forcing himself to turn, he let out a frightened yell. He tried to scramble backwards, but it was too late. There was nowhere to go. He was trapped. For a moment, he thought he would be saved when Brandon saw what was happening. But in the next moment, he remembered he'd turned the camera away towards the wall.

He'd doomed himself.

I can scream. The audio is still working. I can tell them what I'm seeing –

Then everything went black.

CHAPTER TEN

"Look at this room." Sasha said, "It's super creepy. There's an old upside down wheel chair in the corner. And look over there. Is that what I think it is? If I had to guess, I'd say that's an old bed pan." She made a face. "I hope it's empty."

After her confrontation with Todd following Addison's strange behavior in the rec room, Sasha found herself needing to shoulder the bulk of the investigation. Her friend looked exhausted with dark circles under her eyes, and she appeared listless. She wasn't the usually upbeat Addison Sasha knew. In a desperate attempt to get her to engage, she tried once more to drag her friend out of her funk.

"What do you think? Are you picking up on anything right now?"

She was filled with hope when Addison turned and gave her the stink eye. Now *that* was the Addison she knew and loved. Yet as soon as she glared at her friend, she fell back into a wall of silence.

"Addison, why don't you stand here with me? Together we can ask the spirits of the asylum some questions." She thought about the bazillion episodes she'd watched the Ghost Dudes do. Needing to show she knew what she was doing, she cleared her throat and asked the questions the way she'd seen them do it. "Is there anyone here with us? If so, make your presence known."

There was no response.

She continued, "Make a noise if you can. . ."

Again, silence.

Sasha turned to Addison and instantly knew by the look on her face that she was too drained to make any sort of connection.

Thinking on her feet, Sasha changed tactics. "Okay. Since it appears we're not getting much of a response, I'm going to walk the perimeter of the room and just start taking photos. All of you at home, why don't you help us out and keep your eyes peeled because you may catch something we don't."

Sasha started her walk around the room, snapping off pictures as she went. After several clicks and bright flashes, she paused to review the images. "So far, just shots of broken plaster and rotting wood. But never say never." She turned to Todd and smiled. "Let's try this again."

After several more shots, Sasha was once again scrolling through the digital images she'd captured when she suddenly paused. "Wait, I think I got something," She looked down at the digital image on her camera, then up at the wooden panels on the left side of the room. Without a word, she hurried over to one of the panels and began to fiddle with it.

"What are you doing?" Todd asked as he zoomed in closer to capture what Sasha was doing.

"In the photograph, the panel looked out of place. See? It doesn't look as set in the wall as the others." She gave it one last tug and it fell into her hands. Splinters of wood and years of dust filled the air. Between coughs, Sasha exclaimed, "Holy cow. Will you take a look at this? Todd, move in closer. You're going to want to catch this moment on film." She started to reach in when Todd's voice broke through her concentration.

"Don't do that. There could be rats nesting in that hole."

Sasha abruptly pulled her hand back. She looked at him and saw the mischievous smile on his face. "Not funny," she frowned as she reached in again. A moment later, she pulled out what appeared to be an old, leather bound journal.

Barely able to contain her excitement Sasha raced over to a table tucked in the corner of the room. Keeping her in focus, Todd followed close behind.

After wiping her hands against her jeans, she opened the journal and carefully turned the somewhat brittle pages.

"What is it?" Todd asked from behind the camera.

Sasha flipped to the front of the journal. "It says here it's the journal of Dr. Joseph Fisher. Who's he?"

"He was the doctor in charge of the asylum before it closed down."

Sasha jerked her head up and stared at Todd. So he didn't know anything about this place? He was just a cameraman?

She opened her mouth to give him a piece of her mind when she heard Addison's voice beside her. She turned to see her friend leaning over the journal and reading from it.

August 8, 1974. Patient number 492 presented with psychotic episodes. Subdued before undergoing electro shock therapy.

"How horrible," Addison added. She flipped through the pages. "There's more of these kinds of entries." Suddenly, she uttered a small cry and quickly backed away from the table.

"What is it? What's wrong?" Sasha asked.

Addison pointed a shaking finger at the journal. "Near the back. It—it looks like dried blood on the pages."

Sasha's eyes grew wide. She went through the book until she found the dark brown blobs that blocked out several words.

"Shit," she whispered.

"Turn the book towards me so I can get a shot of it," Todd instructed.

She did as he asked and the audience were able to see, for

the first time, one of the last entries made by Dr. Fisher.

October 28th, 1975

I have not wanted to acknowledge the truth, but I have no choice. For the past three years, we have had several patients go missing. I was told it was very possible they wandered off. The asylum is situated on more than twenty acres of dense forest. Searches have been conducted, but no trace has ever been found. Several of the more coherent patients have reported hearing strange noises during the middle of the night on the evenings of the disappearances. One even went so far as to accuse one of my more dedicated orderlies of having something to do with the patients going missing. With nothing but the word of the mentally ill, I had no choice but to set aside their concerns. I strengthened security, but with the state funds we need so desperately to keep this place running being cut back every year, there was only so much I could do.

Yet I now regret my actions. Last night another patient went missing. This one is a twelve year old girl who had been brought in with symptoms of severe schizophrenia. However, when the usual search was conducted, one of the newer orderlies discovered what appears to be human remains in the furnace room.

We are conducting our own internal investigation. We cannot allow this news to get out. The orderly who discovered the remains has been threatened with legal action if he reveals what he found.

We will keep this under wraps for now. We must. Our livelihoods depend on it.

"Quick. Turn the page," Todd commanded.

Sasha did so and Todd again focused the camera on the page.

October 31, 1975

We should have listened to them. We should have heeded their warnings. Because of our arrogance, they had no choice but to take matters into their own hands. The patients are now rioting. As I write this, I can hear their voices as they scream, "Blood for blood." They have blocked the exits. I've hidden myself in my office. I don't know what's going to happen, and I pray to God that I survive this night. But whatever happens, I'm leaving this record as a testament to..."

It was on this page that the blood stains were more prominent. Sasha's heart raced with fear as she and Todd exchanged horrified glances.

"What happened to him?" she forced herself to ask.

"I don't know," he responded. "But that was a great find," he added in an excited voice. "This journal should finally solve the mystery of what happened in Meadowlark Asylum all those years ago."

Sasha felt anything but excited. Yes, it was a terrific find. And it would show how good, if not better The Ghost Seekers were in investigating the paranormal.

But she couldn't erase the shock of seeing the blood on the pages, reading about patients missing, imagining Dr. Fisher holed up in his office, praying for help while the patients bayed for blood and vengeance.

Nor could she erase the thought of the body parts in the furnace room. What had happened in this awful building? And what horror had befallen the twelve year old girl?

"Do you realize that today is the forty-fourth anniversary of the riot?" Todd asked.

"No" she whispered.

Todd turned the camera light towards Addison. "What do you think, Addison?"

The light hit an empty space. She was gone.

"Sasha, grab your flashlight," Todd said as he swung the camera around the room. "She must be in here somewhere."

Sasha's gut churned. She'd been so wrapped up in the journal, she hadn't noticed her friend moving away from the table. She frantically swung her flashlight around the room, but Addison was gone. Her heart hammered in her chest as she thought about her friend, alone somewhere in this vast, frightening building.

Addison, where the hell are you?

***

Addison blinked. And suddenly found herself standing in complete darkness. Her chest tightened and she found herself paralyzed with fear. Despite her ability to see in the dark, she'd never liked the blackness.

With trembling hands, she fumbled for her cellphone and clicked on the flashlight app. A moment later, the light blazed and she saw she was in a room she'd never seen before.

Dear God, what's happening to me?

This was now the third time she'd gone zombie-like. She'd

never experienced anything like that before and it terrified her. It was as if she had no control over her body. Or even her thoughts.

What could have triggered this latest episode? The last thing she remembered was standing next to Sasha, reading the journal.

And the blood. I remember the awful blood on the page –

Suddenly, Addison felt that all-too-familiar sensation overwhelming her. Her skin prickled and her forehead began to tingle.

The air around her swirled and the room took on an ominous feel.

She wanted to run, but her feet were glued to the floor. Anxiety building, she wanted to scream, but the only sound she heard was a keening deep in her throat.

The room seemed to shift, and it was now filled with light. She looked about and felt a shot of fear run down her spine. She knew this room. She'd seen it before.

Oh no. It's the room I saw in my nightmare.

As her gaze swept the room, she saw images slowly materializing. Soon patients appeared sitting at various tables or alone in chairs. The same table and chairs she'd witnessed in her dream. Her legs grew weak when they all turned and stared at her. In the dream, she'd been invisible, but now they could actually see her.

It deepened her fear.

Why am I here? Why is this happening?

The strains of "Stairway to Heaven" began to play, its eerie tune sending shivers throughout her body. It started softly, then grew in intensity. Louder and louder. Addison swiftly covered her ears with her hands, but the song continued, its pounding guitar shattering her mind.

I'm going crazy. I have to get out of here.

But before she could move, she heard the sharp crack of lightning. Blue light filled the room.

Boom!

Thunder rolled overhead.

The floor beneath her feet trembled and shook. Addison instinctively reached out in a desperate attempt to maintain her balance.

A wave of electricity suddenly shot through her. She jerked her hands back to her sides. With fingers still tingling, she involuntarily began clenching and unclenching her fists.

Suddenly the hairs on the back of her neck stood up. She held her breath. Someone was standing right behind her, their hot breath blowing against her skin. Too terrified to look, but equally terrified not to, she forced herself to turn around.

"Hello Addison. I've been waiting for you."

Addison's heart threatened to rip from her chest. The man who had taunted her in her dreams was standing inches from her. His eyes pierced hers, a sadistic smile tugging at the corners of his mouth. She caught her breath when she saw his white orderly's uniform stained with blood.

She was trapped. The only exit was the doorway the man was now blocking. Yet this couldn't be real. None of this was real. Somehow, someway, she must be dreaming again.

Addison pinched her skin, desperate to wake up. But nothing changed. She was still in the room with the music hurting her ears and the man grinning at her. Out of the corner of her eye, she saw the patients lift their arms and point at her.

"Take her! Take her!" they began to chant.

Addison's legs gave out and she fell to her knees. It was no use. She couldn't fight against them. Against him. She was lost. Suddenly, an image of Aunt Juliette appeared in her mind's eye. In her hand, she held a prayer card.

Yes! The prayer of protection she taught me!

She desperately scoured her brain, trying to remember the prayer. But her fear was too great. She was too terrified to think straight.

She closed her eyes tightly and brought her hands together.

Aunt Juliette, please, if you can hear me. I need your help! Please! Help me to remember the prayer! Show me what to do!

Then she waited.

***

Juliette gazed out into the night sky as she washed the last of the dinner dishes. For the better part of the day, she'd been plagued with anxiety, one that appeared to be escalating by the minute. One that left her feeling as if she wanted to jump out of her own skin.

It had started earlier in the day when Addison and Sasha stopped to say goodbye before heading off to meet the van that would take them to wherever they were investigating. Since then, she'd felt guilt-ridden for not trying to do more to convince Addison and her group of friends to turn back before it was too late.

Juliette cringed as she thought of her precocious niece and her Pandora's box of gifts that threatened to burst wide open. Addison had no idea what she was getting herself into. And every time she thought about The Ghost Dudes and their fear factor mentality, her anxiety only heightened. Juliette groaned inwardly.

I should have told Addison the truth.

But what could she do? She'd made a promise to her twin sister Anne years ago never to tell Addison about the gypsy blood that ran deep and strong in the women of their family. The blood that gave them their gifts. Given the sisters' strained relationship, Juliette felt obligated to approach Addison's questions with caution, even as every fiber of her being longed to be honest with the young girl.

She smiled sadly when she recalled her youth. Poor Anne had tried so desperately to block out the voices of the dead that plagued her. She'd even gone as far as turning up the radio to ear splitting volumes to block them out.

Juliette recognized that Anne had gotten her fear from their mother. Calling their gifts 'the family curse', the older woman handed out vials of holy water as if it was candy. She often turned a deaf ear to sudden outbursts of strange laughter that emanated from Anne's room at all hours of the night.

Juliette, on the other hand, had chosen to embrace her gifts. To let go and accept who and what she was. It hadn't always been easy living an authentic life as a psychic medium, but it provided her with a peace that couldn't be bought.

Now, rife with a tension she couldn't quite understand, she picked up the last of the dinner plates and allowed her mind to wander.

Addison, wherever you are, I pray you are safe.

The plate slid out of her hand and crashed in the sink when she abruptly felt an energy she'd never felt before swarm over her. The hair on her neck and arms stood on end as the kitchen became charged with static electricity.

What is that? Who is that?

Juliette cautiously opened herself up.

Crack!

A shot of energy ran through her that sent her stumbling against the sink.

Aunt Juliette...

She caught her breath. "Addison?" she cried out as her gaze darted around the room.

As she struggled to comprehend what was happening, Juliette abruptly felt herself overcome with a fear so sharp, it almost brought her to her knees. Her hand flew to her heart as it suddenly became crystal clear.

"She's in danger! My baby is in danger!"

As soon as she spoke, another energy came in. Instead of fear, her skin now prickled with danger. Malevolence.

Evil.

Juliette felt herself sliding into panic. In all her years of interacting with the paranormal, she'd never encountered an energy so dark and debilitating.

She fought to tamp down her terror. Whatever this was, she couldn't let it win. Addison needed her.

Knowing that fear would only feed this dark entity, she struggled to calm herself. To ease her racing heart and regain her breath. Grounding herself, she was finally regaining control over her emotions when she heard a voice that sent her back to the edge of panic.

Aunt Juliette, if you can hear me. I need your help! Please! Help me to remember the protection prayer! Show me…"

Although Juliette couldn't see him, she suddenly felt a male presence standing between her and Addison. Her fear turned to anger as she perceived his joy at hurting. Maiming. Bullying.

"You will not win," she yelled out.

Her mind filled with sinister laugher. He was mocking her. Trying to bend her to his will.

Instead of giving in, Juliette hurried to the cabinet where she kept her quartz crystals. Gathering the larger ones in her hands, she sat down at the kitchen table. Blocking out the laughter as much as she could, she worked quickly to create a circular grid on the tablecloth. When she was done, she held her hands over it and closed her eyes.

"I'm here, baby girl. Listen to my voice and feel my strength."

Juliette brought up an image of Addison in her mind's eye. Love filled her as she thought about this precious girl who was such a light in her life. The more she filled herself with love, the more she was able to send that love to Addison. Slowly, she felt the presence begin to back off.

Darkness is simply an absence of light. And my love for Addison is the brightest light there is.

"Addison, don't be afraid," she whispered under her breath. "That will only strengthen him. Be strong, my girl. I know you have it in you. Now, repeat after me…"

She visualized the words and directed them at her niece. As she did so, she also sent calming energy in an effort to quiet Addison's fears.

Archangel Michael. Defend us in battle. Be our protection against the malice and snares of the devil…

She murmured the prayer over and over, hoping she wasn't too late.

***

Addison was at her lowest. She was exhausted. Her energy was gone. She felt completely helpless. She had nothing left in her to combat the darkness that was slowly consuming her.

Addison, I'm here. Aunt Juliette is here. Listen to me carefully. You cannot be afraid. Your fear only makes him stronger. Repeat after me the words of the St. Michael's Prayer of Protection. Do that for me now.

Words flooded into her mind. As if grasping for a lifeline, Addison pushed through the fog in her brain and repeated the powerful words.

"Archangel Michael. Defend us in battle… "

Addison chanted the prayer over and over again. As she did so, she was surprised to feel another energy now surround her – an energy of love and light.

And safety.

With each recitation, she watched as the patients slowly receded back into the shadows, their shouts fading away. The music ceased playing, and she felt her strength returning.

Forcing herself to look up, she saw Gerald's expression change from one of triumph to one of rage.

"We're not done yet," he spat out before disappearing into the darkness of the hallway.

Addison closed her eyes and tried her best to calm her beating heart. She still sensed him around, but he felt far away. Far enough away that he was no longer overshadowing her with his foul presence.

Opening her eyes, she found herself back in the darkness. The light that had illuminated the room was gone, sending it back to its present state of neglect and abandonment.

She wasn't sure what had happened, but she knew her aunt had saved her life.

Thank you, Aunt Juliette. I am forever grateful.

She took a deep breath, releasing it slowly as she reached out to test the mental link she'd felt with her aunt. But that familiar, tingling sensation she'd felt a short while ago was gone.

Addison slowly climbed to her feet. Covered with dust from the floor, she brushed away at her jeans, her mind filled with what had just happened. Suddenly, and without warning, she felt a pair of icy hands grab her around her waist.

Oh God, he's back!

Addison let out a piercing scream.

CHAPTER ELEVEN

"Addison, it's me! Hey, girlfriend, it's Sasha!"

Struggling to free herself, it took a few moments for Addison to recognize Sasha's concerned face staring back at her. Relief flooded her as she threw her arms around the Latina's shoulders.

"Oh, thank God it's you," she exclaimed.

"Who else would it be?"

Addison took a step back and looked at Todd and Sasha. "What happened?" she asked. "How did I end up in this room?"

"You tell me. One minute you were standing next to me in the break room and the next minute you're gone. You just about gave us a heart attack." Sasha gave her friend a stern look. "You can't go disappearing like that, Addy. This place is beyond weird. Not to mention dangerous what with loose plaster, broken glass and floors we can fall through."

Sasha took in Addison's ashen features. What frightened her more was the glazed look in the young woman's eyes. Her anger at Addison's sudden disappearance melted away, replaced by deep concern.

"It's going to be okay. Let's get you back to basecamp."

"It's not going to be okay. Not as long as we stay here." Her eyes bored into Sasha's. "This building wants to kill us. *He* wants to kill us."

"Who are you talking about?"

"Him."

"Him who?"

"I don't know."

They were interrupted when Levi, followed by Mark and Devon burst into the room.

"Are you alright?" Devon asked as he came up to Addison. "We watched the commotion on the monitor when Sasha and Todd realized you'd disappeared." Before she could respond, he turned to Sasha. "Fantastic job finding that journal."

Ignoring the fact that Todd was probably still filming them, Sasha stomped over to Devon and stuck her finger in his face. "No more bullshit," she snapped. "And no more lies. You're going to tell us right here, right now about the riot that took place on October 31, 1975. And you're going to tell us who or what the Monster of the Asylum is."

Devon smiled. "Now Sasha, that's part of the reveal at the end of the show."

"Oh yeah? Well, if you don't come clean, my team is leaving, but not before we all shove your reveal up your ass."

Devon's smile faltered slightly. Once again, he felt the investigation slipping out of his control. He had to do something to assert his authority.

He turned to Todd and the camera.

"How about it, you guys watching at home? Are you ready to find out the truth about the ghostly monster who lurks in the Meadowlark Asylum?"

Standing off camera, Mark looked down at his iPhone, saw the audience response and gave the thumbs up.

"Mark," Devon continued. "Radio Tina and ask her to meet us up here. In the meantime, tell us what you saw, Addison. I'm sure the people at home would like to know what made you walk away from Sasha and Todd."

Ten minutes later Tina arrived to find Addison trying her best to find words to describe what she'd experienced. She instantly knew the young woman wasn't telling the whole story, but she was sharing enough to keep Devon and the audience at home happy.

"Did you actually see the presence that summoned you to this room?" Devon asked.

She nodded. "He looked like some sort of nurse. A male nurse. His white uniform was stained with blood." She paused to take a deep breath and let it out slowly. "I—I think his name is Gerald. There's a darkness in him. An evil that's so…" she shuddered, unable to go on. Levi immediately came up next to her and put a reassuring arm around her shoulder.

Devon nodded. "You're about to find out what an understatement that really is, Addison." He turned and saw Tina on the edge of the group. "Ah, Tina's just arrived. It's time for me to tell the story of the Meadowlark Asylum."

He positioned himself in the center of the small group and looked into the camera.

"Addison is absolutely correct in describing the male orderly she saw as a person who was evil. In fact, we now believe he was a sociopath. Although the records from this time period were destroyed years ago when the asylum was closed, from what we were able to pull together, we think his name was Gerald Harper." Devon took a dramatic step towards the camera. "And it appears he was a serial killer of epic proportions."

Tina felt a sudden chill run down her spine. She glanced at Addison and saw the young woman felt it too. As Devon continued to describe Gerald Harper, the room grew colder. A malevolent energy soon made itself known, its frigid breath blowing against the back of Tina's neck.

Addison watched the color drain from Tina's face. She jumped slightly when she felt an ice-cold finger slide against her cheek.

He's here. Gerald Harper is here. And I'm not the only one feeling his presence.

She'd had enough. She couldn't take this anymore. If they didn't get out of there, Harper was going to add several more victims to his list. She opened her mouth to protest but Tina beat her to it.

"Stop!" Tina shouted as she pushed her way to Devon and put her hand up. "He's here, Devon. Gerald is here. He doesn't want his secrets revealed. He's going to hurt someone if you continue."

Devon turned and looked at Tina. This was better than he could have hoped for. It was plain to see how terrified she was. And that garbage about Harper being here? That was priceless. The audience had to be eating all this up.

"What exactly are you feeling, Tee?"

She stared at him in disbelief. "You don't feel that?" Before he could answer, she swung around to Mark. "Are you feeling anything?"

Mark nodded. "I feel as though I want to jump out of my skin."

"Me too!" Levi added. "Like someone just draped a heavy blanket over me."

"That's his nasty energy surrounding us. We need to be careful," Tina continued. "He's going to do whatever it takes to make sure his secrets don't come out."

Devon reached out and grabbed the journal out of Sasha's jacket pocket.

"Sasha was led to this journal for a reason. We owe it to our viewers to at least share some of what is in here."

"That's not a good idea," Tina warned.

He pointedly ignored her as he opened the journal and flipped through it. "Here's an entry from October 30, 1975. That's one day before the riots that forced the authorities to close this place down." He cleared his throat and began to read aloud.

I still can't believe what Police Chief O'Neil revealed to me during our meeting today. Was I so lost in my work that I didn't even notice what was going on outside these walls? Between the fall of 1969 and the spring of 1972, ten people disappeared from the surrounding area. Chief O'Neil now believes the culprit was someone within these walls. I had Mary pull the files on the disappearing patients and I am sick over my suspicions. They began disappearing soon after the killings stopped in Ashboro. Chief O'Neil is convinced one person is responsible for both the killings in Ashboro and the disappearances here at Meadowlark. There were only two orderlies hired in 1969 --

Suddenly, the journal was ripped from Devon's hands and flung across the room where it hit the wall and fell to the floor. Sasha hurried over and swooped it up in her grasp.

"Unbelievable! Did you see that?" Devon shouted to the camera gleefully.

"He's not kidding," Tina implored. "Please. Don't read anymore. We need to get out of here now!"

Her voice had risen several octaves, and it was obvious how frightened she was.

"Sure, sure. We'll gather back at basecamp and plan our next move."

"There isn't going to be a next move—" She was cut off when Devon signaled to Todd to turn off the camera. When the red light went off, he turned to the group. "Why don't you guys return to basecamp? Tina and I will be right behind you."

He grabbed her elbow and held her tightly as the group left the room. Once they were alone, he turned to her.

"I've had it. You do not argue with me on camera."

"I'll argue with you wherever and whenever I have to in order for you to see reason. Your head is so up your ass over ratings, you're endangering all of us. The sad part is, you don't even give a shit about us. You'd be happy to film us dying so you can get to your precious number one spot!"

Devon's face turned red with rage. "That's it. You're gone, Tina. When we finish here tonight, I'm finding another psychic. In fact, I'm going to offer the position to Addison. She's obviously a better psychic than you could ever hope to be."

"You're despicable. And if we make it out of here alive, you don't need to fire me. I quit."

She turned on her heel and hurried from the room. Devon watched her go, furious at her behavior, yet glad he wouldn't need to deal with her anymore in the future. She was one problem he was happy to be done with.

Taking a deep breath, he shook off his frustration. There were still some things he needed to get done - things that were going to blow this investigation into the stratosphere. But he had to hurry. He didn't have much time left to set into motion his masterpiece.

***

Tina's hands shook from anger and frustration. This investigation was way out of their league. They'd never encountered anything like this before, and she felt like a lamb being led to the slaughter. The evil, the danger she'd witnessed in that room when Devon was reading from the journal was beyond anything she's ever experienced before. She had to get out of here. She had to get those kids out of here. This went beyond TV ratings. This was about their very lives.

She needed to think. To wrap her mind around the next steps she needed to take to save them from the hands of a ghost they had no defense against. She reached the foyer, but instead of turning towards basecamp, she scurried down the hall and into what had once been a visitors' bathroom. There, she leaned up against the sink and stared at herself in the aged, filmy mirror.

"I don't care about the network. I don't care about Devon. I don't care about this damned house. I'm going to gather whoever wants to come with me and get them out to one of the vans where we can drive as far away from this place as possible."

Tina rubbed her weary eyes and was about to turn away when she caught something out of the corner of her eye. Glancing back at her reflection, she gasped when she saw the image of another woman staring back at her.

She was young, with long blonde hair that was knotted and unkempt. She wore a hospital gown stained with food. She'd been beautiful once, but her incarceration in the asylum had left her face worn and filled with despair.

Tina stood mesmerized by the woman. She physically felt the patient's sadness, depression. It was as though a weight had settled in her chest as she took on the image's emotions.

"Who are you?" Tina whispered.

There was no response. The woman continued to silently stare at her. Her emotions washed over Tina until she thought her heart would break as she experienced the apparition's hopelessness.

Before she realized what she was doing, Tina lifted her hand and rested it against the glass.

"Let me help you. You don't need to stay here anymore. You are free to continue your soul journey."

The woman opened her mouth to gasp her surprise. As if she'd heard Tina's comforting words and realized, for the first time, she didn't need to stay. Tina felt her heart leap in happiness as she saw an opportunity to actually help a lost soul rather than just capture its voice on an EVP, or its shadow on camera. Maybe she could help her escape this hellhole and the horror that was Gerald Harper.

Her happiness however, quickly turned to puzzlement as she watched the woman's mouth grow longer and longer until her jaw was nearly down to her chest. The sad brown eyes shriveled up back into her head, leaving two black gaping holes staring back at Tina.

Suddenly, a skeletal hand reached out through the mirror and grabbed Tina's wrist. She uttered a strangled scream and pulled back, but the grip on her was too strong. She felt herself being pulled towards the mirror while she desperately fought to pull away. In her struggle to break free, Tina had the stark realization that if she went through the glass, she'd be gone forever.

Frantic, and with no other means of escape, Tina balled her hand into a fist and hurled it against the glass, shattering it into large shards. The thing abruptly released its grip on her and she fell back against one of the stall doors. Despite her knuckles bleeding, Tina struggled to regain her footing and ran out of the bathroom.

Terrified, her only thought to flee the building, Tina dashed to the front door, flung it open and sprinted out into the night.

The air was cold, and the moonlight threw off long, deep shadows as she ran towards one of the vans. Grabbing the handle, she tried to open it only to cry out in frustration when she realized it was locked. Panicking now, only one idea stood out. She had to get off the grounds. She had to put as much distance as she could between herself and that cursed building.

Tina turned and darted down the driveway towards the front gates. As she ran, she thought of the teenagers. She couldn't leave them. But, oh God, she couldn't go back to that building. She just couldn't.

I swear, I'll find help. Somehow, someway, I'll bring back the authorities and get you all out of there.

The night air chilled her as she rushed along the road. The moonlight helped illuminate her way as her breathing filled her ears. Thank goodness she was an avid jogger. She'd be able to cover the mile to the front gates without much trouble before heading towards Ashboro. She didn't relish running alone in an area she wasn't familiar with, but with the horrors of the asylum at her heels fueling her forward, she deliberately blocked out her fears.

Tina had gotten into that almost hypnotic state she achieved whenever she hit her rhythm, when she became aware of a strange energy surrounding her. Not sure what she was feeling, she glanced towards the woods.

And instantly regretted it.

Figures were emerging from the thick underbrush. Most were dressed in the ragged remains of hospital gowns. Her heart almost stopped when she saw several that resembled the charred remains of what had once been human beings.

This is impossible! They can't be real.

But the cacophony of moans that filled the night air warned her that they were very real. And they were heading towards her.

Hoping to outrun them, Tina increased her speed. Another half mile, and she'd be through the gates and away from this nightmare.

Her hopes were dashed when she came out of a curve in the road and saw what appeared to be hundreds of the vile things blocking her way.

Oh no, oh no, oh no.

She stopped short on the driveway and immediately heard her mind attacked by a symphony of cries and pleas for help. She clamped her hands over her ears, but they wouldn't stop their assault on her sanity. In the midst of the incessant wailing, she heard a voice that almost sent her over the edge.

You belong to us, Tina. We have a place for you right beside us. You're one of us now.

She shrank back as she watch the group turn towards her in unison and outstretch their arms, summoning her forward. Into their decaying embrace.

Thrown into a full blown panic, Tina blindly veered to her right. Not caring where she was running, her only thought was to survive.

Sobbing now, Tina blindly raced forward. She sprinted through a row of shrubs that tore at her jacket. Her screams echoed in the night, convinced the branches were hands trying to grab onto her.

She whimpered in terror as the moans from the patients quickly turned into peals of laughter, swooping in and attacking her from all sides. The trees closed in on her, their dark limbs blocking out the moonlight and plunging her into a thick blackness that increased her panic.

With fear now in control, Tina continued her panicked run through the woods. She had enough sense left, however, to notice a stone wall that suddenly loomed up in front of her. Thankfully, she saw it at the last moment and managed to leap over the low structure. Her elation that she'd cleared it quickly turned to alarm when, instead of hitting the ground on the other side, she felt herself plunging into a deep hole.

Her last thought before she hit the bottom was the realization that she'd fallen into an open grave.

Tina smashed her forehead into the cold, hard ground, her mouth and nostrils filled with dirt.

She groaned as she felt something wet drip down into her eyes and mouth.

It was blood.

"Help me," she whispered, but the words sounded barely audible and far away. With consciousness flickering in and out, it took her a long moment to sense the patients surrounding the edge of the grave. When she did, she tried to scream, but it came out as a hoarse croak. The last tenuous hold on her sanity broke when she realized they were throwing dirt down onto her motionless body.

They're going to bury me alive.

Then everything went black.

***

Devon was incensed. Seeing that Tina hadn't followed the group into basecamp, he went out in search of her and immediately saw the front door wide open.

Shit! She really did leave just as she'd threatened. His first thought was how this was going to affect the show. But it wasn't long before his mind spun a story that would make a dramatic night even more dramatic.

This place is so frightening, so horrifying that Tina could no longer deal with the onslaught of evil that stalks its halls. For the sake of her safety and sanity, we had one of our technicians take her off the premises so she could recover from her terrifying ordeal.

That sounded good. He'd probably tweak it a bit more before he returned to basecamp and made the announcement.

Besides, Addison was more than a match for Tina. In fact, she was ten times better than Tina. She had just the right amount of drama and tension they'd been lacking. And she was extremely photogenic.

Good-bye, Tina. Hello Addison.

***

"I say we pull the plug on this shitshow and get the hell out of here," Sasha whispered to Addison and Levi just before they entered basecamp.

"How do we get out of here?" Levi asked. "You think they're just going to let us waltz off with one of their vans?"

"We're not waltzing off," Sasha replied calmly. "We're borrowing. They've got enough lackeys who can come pick it up later."

"What about our contract? We can't afford to have the network sue us for walking out."

Sasha turned to Addison. "What does your otherworldly senses say? Should we stick it out, or leave before the gates of hell completely open up and suck us in?"

Addison felt a shiver run down her spine. She glanced at the staircase that stood behind them and had a sense of several spirits standing there. She couldn't see them, but she could feel them. Watching. Waiting to see what they'd do.

"I say we go. The sooner we get out of here, the safer we'll all be."

"I'll get Stan."

"What if Devon or Brandon try to stop you?" Addison asked.

Sasha gave her a slight smile. "Let me worry about that."

After she'd gone, Levi threw Addison a concerned look.

"I didn't like the sound of that," he admitted.

"We're out of options here. Better Sasha causes some trouble than this building killing us."

Levi's eyes widened. "You really think it would come to that?"

Addison nodded. "Oh yeah. Aunt Juliette warned me we shouldn't play around with the paranormal. She was right. There's evil in here, Levi. And I have absolutely no idea how to deal with it."

Knowing Addison was not a woman given to theatrics or unnecessary drama, he felt afraid for the first time. It was at that moment Sasha came hurrying back. He could tell right away by her demeanor that something was terribly wrong. Which only deepened his fear.

"Brandon said Stan went off to the bathroom ten minutes ago. He was so busy with the monitors he didn't realize he hadn't returned until I showed up."

"Damn," Levi said. He ran outside and was soon back.

"He's not in the porta-potty."

"Crap," Sasha muttered. "We're not leaving without him. But where the hell can he be?"

***

"Ugh," Stan mumbled as his eyelids flickered open. "What the –" He tried to sit up only to smash his head against what appeared to be a ceiling. A very low ceiling. He fell back and took notice of his surroundings for the first time.

It was pitch black wherever he was. Something that sent his heart hammering in terror. He'd never liked the dark. Nor did he like enclosed places. They'd always creeped him out, sending his imagination into overdrive.

Reaching up with his hands and feeling his way around what seemed to be cold steel, he realized to his horror that he was in a space so confining he couldn't turn onto his side. What frightened him even more was the overwhelming smell of rot and decay filling his nostrils.

"Help!" he shouted as he banged against the steel with his fists. "Help!"

But his words echoed back at him.

Don't panic. Don't panic.

But he was panicking. His terror increased when, through his escalating emotions, he heard the unmistakable sounds of whispers coming at him from all sides.

This can't be happening. It can't.

But it was. He couldn't make out the words, but they were closing in on him, their indistinguishable murmurs fanning his increasing fear.

"Help!" he screamed as he found himself falling to pieces.

His terror exploded when he suddenly realized he couldn't catch his breath.

Shit! I'm suffocating!

Flailing his arms and legs around in desperation, he found his lungs closing.

Until there was barely any air left.

CHAPTER TWELVE

"I don't get it. I can't see Stan running off by himself. Do you?" Levi gave an exasperated sigh, staring intently at Sasha and Addison as he waited for a reply.

The two shook their heads in response.

"I don't have a good feeling about this," Sasha said as she glanced over her shoulder at the staircase. "There's something totally weird about Stan's disappearance. And with all this talk about the Monster of the Asylum and what Addison's been experiencing, it's creeping me the hell out. I thought The Ghost Dudes made all this shit up for publicity. But after finding the journal, I don't know what to think."

Overcome with sudden emotion, Sasha turned away from Levi and Addison to flick away tears forming in the corners of her eyes. "I'm sorry I got you all into this. I never thought it would be like this. What if Stan is really in trouble? It'll be all my fault."

Levi, uncomfortable with Sasha's uncharacteristic display, gently punched her in the shoulder. "Come on Sash. Don't lose it now. We need you." He motioned toward Addison who nodded her head in agreement. "Besides, none of us could have predicted this. We all thought we'd be investigating some cheesy haunted house, not a mental asylum that likes to eat people."

Sasha chuckled. "You're right Levi. You *do* need me."

Levi rolled his eyes, but the joke helped ease the tension.

She threw back her shoulders. "We're not going to find Stan standing here feeling sorry for ourselves. Stan the Man needs us."

Addison spoke up. "Maybe we should check with Brandon again to see if he's been able to locate Stan on the monitors."

"I guess that makes sense," Levi said.

Going back inside, both Mark and Brandon swore they hadn't seen anything, while Devon downplayed their concern.

"I'm sure he got bored and decided to stretch his legs. He'll be back before you know it."

Livid at his indifference, Sasha started towards him to rip him a new one when Levi pulled her back.

"No time," he whispered.

Realizing he was right – Stan was somewhere in this building and could be in real danger - Sasha reluctantly allowed the others to lead her back into the foyer.

To their surprise, Mark emerged from basecamp and joined them.

"Your friend really doesn't give a shit about anything, does he?" Sasha retorted.

"It's not that. It's just that he—" Mark left the sentence hanging. It had taken him a long time to face the painful truth, but Sasha was right. Devon was only interested in Devon and in the show. Instead, he said, "Look, I don't like the idea of Stan being on his own in this place any more than you do. I'm also a bit worried Tina didn't come back with us to basecamp. I'm going to check around upstairs. The two of them may have decided to do a bit of investigating on their own."

"Stan would never do that," Addison replied firmly.

Mark stared at her for a long moment before turning and disappearing up the stairs.

"Well, that sounded totally bogus," Sasha said in disgust.

Addison shivered outwardly and zipped her dark purple jacket up as high as it would go. "I hope we find him soon," she replied. "I don't know about you two, but it feels like the temperature is dropping by the minute."

Sasha and Levi gave Addison a worried look.

"It's been cold in here all day," Levi pointed out.

Rubbing her hands briskly together, she said, "This isn't just *cold*. It's like an inside-my-body cold. You know what I mean?"

Levi looked slightly dumbfounded as Sasha, pushing aside her concerns, replied, "Like I said before, the quicker we find Stan, the sooner we can get out of here." She turned to Addison. "I'll make you a deal. You put that psychic thinking cap on and I'll treat you to a round of hot chocolate later. I'll even spring for salted caramel flavoring. That'll warm you up big time."

Psychic thinking cap?

"You're already proven how psychic you are," Sasha continued. "Maybe there's a way you can direct it. You know, like driving a car. See if you can put out your antenna and *feel* where Stan is."

Addison frowned at her. "I'm not an insect."

"But you sense things. Maybe you can sense Stan. It's either that or we waste precious time checking out this entire building. That will take hours and if Stan is in trouble, or injured..."

"Just focus on Stan and see what you get," Levi urged. "It won't hurt to try."

Addison looked into their faces. She too was frightened that Stan was missing. For his sake, she had to attempt to use whatever abilities she seemed to have to find him.

Releasing a breath she hadn't realized she was holding, she closed her eyes. She brought up an image of Stan in her mind's eye and held it in place. She thought back to the afternoon when she and her friends had approached Stan for the first time and asked him to join their team. She recalled their hands touching and the strange sensation that shot up between the two of them. The memory was working. His image became sharper, more vibrant. So close she could almost make out the small smattering of freckles on the bridge of his nose.

Her forehead tingled. It was the same sensation she'd felt upstairs. Only this time, there was no malevolence involved.

Stan, where are you? Show me, please!

The image of Stan in her mind's eye slowly changed. He was no longer smiling at her. He now seemed to be staring into the darkness. Into an abyss.

But where? Where is he?

Breathing in sharply, she received her answer as she felt the first pull of energy, jerking her to the right.

Turning towards the energy that beckoned to her, Addison nearly cried out as the intensity of Stan's fear washed over her. With her heart threatening to rip through her chest, she found it difficult to catch her breath. She raised her hand to her heart in an effort to ease the pain, but the inability to breathe grew until she thought she would pass out.

Her hands ached as she felt the sensation of pounding her fists against a hard, cold surface.

Addison gasped as she was hit with a sudden sense of urgency. Time was running out for Stan. They needed to find him NOW.

But where was he?

She needed to focus. If she couldn't, he'd die.

She closed her eyes and fought to rebalance herself. She pushed aside her fears and forced herself to keep her attention solely on the image of Stan she'd brought up in her mind's eye. It wasn't long before she felt again a pull to her right, as if someone were tugging at her from that direction. She opened her eyes and walked towards the energy. To her surprise, she saw a door tucked beneath the staircase.

"Where does that lead?" she asked.

"I think that's the door to the basement," Levi answered.

Addison grabbed the door handle and swung it open. "Follow me."

***

They called him The Monster of the Asylum.

How he'd come to love that name.

When he was alive, he'd had to pretend he had compassion for his charges. He could never reveal how much he loathed their whining, and crying and moaning. It was only when night fell that he could discard the pretense and become who he truly was. It was his favorite part of the day – taking his time picking just the right one for his cat and mouse game. It had to be one that challenged his intellect. It wouldn't do if the mouse contained the mental capacity of a gnat.

He often thought of those poor idiots. Just as he'd controlled them in life within these walls, he now controlled them in death. He still had the capacity to lure them from their rooms with promises he had no intention of fulfilling.

Even after all these years, they still remained desperate for relief.

Yet they were no longer fulfilling. No. He'd learned to wait patiently for a new set of idiots who dared enter his domain. And, like clockwork, they always arrived. Hungry for answers.

Answers he was all too willing to provide.

And here they were again. Another group of fools. Oh, how he was enjoying them. There were two who particularly interested him. He felt his excitement growing at the thought of once again resurrecting his favorite game.

It had been ten years since he'd been able to play it. Before this night was over, he'd play it again. With relish. And joy.

And with the knowledge that this was a game he never, ever lost.

***

Addison, flashlight in hand, led the way down the stairs

and stopped short. Sasha and Levi, following close behind, crashed into her.

"Which way now?" Levi asked as they found themselves standing in the middle of a hallway. To the left lay what appeared to be the older part of the hospital. The floors were made of concrete, and the walls were thick with mildew. Here and there, water trickled down the walls and pooled into large puddles. To the right, the floors and walls were tiled and appeared to be in much better shape.

Sasha poked her head out from the group and looked up and down the corridor. "Stan would never have gone down here by himself. I know I said you were psychic Addison, but is this really what you saw?"

Despite the decreasing temperatures in the cold, dank basement, the flashlight slipped out of Addison's damp, sweaty palms.

Levi caught it and gave it back to her. "Be careful. If the flashlight breaks, we'll be finding our way back in the dark."

"What about our phones?" Sasha asked in a shaky voice.

"Mine's pretty much dead. And I'd be surprised if we can get a signal down here." He turned to Addison. "Where now?"

She glanced to her right, then back to her left. Closing her eyes, she focused her thoughts on Stan. She felt an immediate tug to her left. "I think I feel him down there."

"Of course it has to be down the creepier end of the corridor," Sasha groaned in disgust.

They were about to start walking when they heard a loud banging echoing down the hallway. Each stopped and gasped aloud.

Bang, bang, bang

"What the hell is that?" Sasha asked in fear. The banging sound echoed again. "What if it's that Monster of the Asylum trying to lure us to our death?"

"What if it's Stan trying to get help?"

Still none of them moved. Addison closed her eyes again

and concentrated. To her surprise, she found her breathing even more labored.

"Stan is in real trouble," she gasped for breath between words.

"Come on," Levi urged. "I'll go first. You two get behind me."

Grabbing back the flashlight from Addison, they hurried down the hall, ignoring the water splashing up over their boots and jeans from the murky, mold filled puddles.

They stopped at the first door. Sasha pointed up to the rusted sign above the doorway and gulped.

"It's the morgue," she whispered. She turned to Addison. "You think he's in there?"

Addison nodded.

Cringing at the shrill sound of rusted metal against metal, they watched as Levi struggled to open the heavy door.

"Hurry," Addison whispered. "He's suffocating."

Urged on by her warning, Levi finally managed to get the door open. They stumbled into the room where he shone the beam around the large, rectangular room.

"Stan, are you in here?" he called out.

The beam of light fell onto a stainless steel table that stood in the middle of the room. It had grooves along the edges and a block protruding near the top. They all caught their breath as they recognized it as the table on which autopsies were once performed.

Swinging the flashlight again, they saw the far wall lined with row after row of large square drawers.

Addison's blood ran cold as her mind took in their surroundings.

Dear God. Stan is here. I can feel him. But where?

Suddenly she felt a sudden surge of energy blanket her. It was filled with terror and the realization of impending death. It took her a few moments to realize Stan's energy was blending with her own.

Her chest was on fire. She'd run out of air. She could no longer breathe.

Shit! He's dying!

Addison suddenly found herself in a small enclosed space. Her leg muscles were cramped, and she was surrounded by total darkness.

"He's in there!" she screamed as she pointed to the metal drawers.

Sasha and Levi ran forward and frantically opened each one, their only light coming from the flashlight in Levi's hand.

The sound of clanging, metal drawers rapidly opening and closing filled the silence.

"He's in here," Sasha cried out as she opened a drawer and saw a head of brown hair lying still. "Quick, help me get him out."

Overcome with relief that he'd been found, and realizing she could now breathe, Addison ran to help Sasha and Levi maneuver the table out from the confined space.

Her happiness quickly evaporated when she saw Stan's pale face caked in blood. She pushed past her friends and grabbed his shoulders. "Stan, wake up. Please don't be dead. Stan!"

He remained motionless.

A sudden thought popped into Addison's mind. What did she have to lose? "Come back to us, Stan!" she wailed as she pulled her arm back and slapped him sharply across the face.

Stan took a sharp intake of breath.

Opening his eyes, he slowly turned his head towards Addison.

"Did you just hit me?"

"Stan, I'm so sorry, I—"

"I can't believe you just hit me."

Despite his words, he plastered a shaky smirk on his face.

He's going to be okay. Addison placed a trembling hand over her heart and sighed with relief. *Thank God.*

Between the three of them, they hoisted Stan out from the drawer. He was drenched in sweat, and despite his bravado, he was visibly trembling.

"You okay, man? You scared the living daylights out of us," Levi said as he helped Stan to his feet. Weakened by his terrifying experience, Stan's knees buckled. Levi quickly caught him and wrapped one of Stan's arms around his shoulder.

"You're safe now," he replied in encouragement.

"How the hell did you end up in the morgue of all places?" Sasha asked as she motioned to the wall of drawers.

In a raspy voice, Stan spat out, "Devon."

They gasped in disbelief.

"Are you sure? Why on earth would he do that?" Sasha asked.

Stan struggled to catch his breath. "Sorry, I was suffocating in there. Just give me a few here."

He took several deep breaths before he felt himself able to continue. "He's been staging everything. While I was manning the monitors, I noticed something odd when a chair moved on its own during one of Devon's solo investigations. When I went to check it out, I found a wire tied to the chair leg. Devon must have snuck up behind me because before I could say or do anything, he knocked me out. The next thing I remember I was—" He hesitated, then jerked his head towards the drawers. "—in there." He shivered involuntarily at the memory. "Thank God, you guys found me, I thought I was going to die." He glanced at his friends. "By the way, how did you find me?"

Levi pointed to Addison. "She's psychic, remember?"

He turned a stunned face towards her. "Really? You found me using your abilities?"

She blushed.

"What a screw-up this whole experience has been," Sasha snapped. "We should have known The Ghost Dudes were nothing but a bunch of frauds."

Addison's chest tightened in fear as she suddenly felt an unfamiliar energy enter the room. "We can argue about that later. Right now, we need to get out of here," she said.

"I'm with you. This place is all kinds of bad." Levi threw a worried look at his friends, "And now that we know Devon actually tried to *murder* Stan, he'll never let us out of here alive."

"We need to stick to Plan A," Sasha replied.

"Which is?"

"We get out of this building without being seen. We then grab one of the vans and drive out of here like a bat out of hell."

"Sounds good to me," Stan concurred.

They all started towards the door.

"We can't leave," Addison suddenly whispered.

They stopped short and stared at her.

"Why?" Sasha asked.

"Because there's someone blocking the doorway."

CHAPTER THIRTEEN

Stan, Levi and Sasha looked at each other in bewilderment. There was no one standing in the doorway – at least no one they could see. But Addison was staring ahead, the expression on her face clearly indicating she was seeing someone.

"Levi," Sasha whispered. "Find some kind of weapon. If it's Devon out there—"

"It's not Devon," Addison replied as she suddenly broke away from the group and moved towards the door. "It's a little girl."

"Did you put something in her soda?" Sasha asked, giving Stan a side glance.

"She's psychic, remember?" he countered. "She has the ability to reach beyond our physical realm to the plane where spirits and other things unseen by the human eye exist."

"The only part I understood of what you just said was 'other things'," Levi responded. "And I don't think I want to understand that."

"Shhh," Sasha admonished him. "Addison knows we need to get out of here. The only reason she's not running out that door is because she really is seeing something. We have no choice but to follow her lead on this."

Levi sighed. "I liked her better when all she did was find wedding rings in softball fields."

While the group whispered among themselves, Addison slowly approached the young girl plainly standing in the doorway. In her small hand dangled a teddy bear that had seen better days. It looked motheaten and was torn in several places, but it was obvious it meant a great deal to the youngster.

She looked to be no more than twelve years old. Her hospital gown was yellowed with dirt and age, and her large hollowed out eyes - eyes that had seen too much for a girl her age – continued to steadily watch Addison. Her dark greasy hair hung down her back and the sight of its' tangles and knots broke Addison's heart. She loved brushing Kylie's blonde curls and the sight of this neglected, emaciated child was almost too much to bear.

"I'm Addison," she said in a low voice as she knelt down in front of the girl.

The girl said nothing. Instead, she reached out and grasped Addison's hand in hers. The teenager swallowed a gasp as she felt the icy touch of the apparition's fingers wrapped around hers. The girl tugged at her, obviously wanting Addison to follow her. Caught up in what she was experiencing, the teenager stood up and allowed the apparition to lead her out of the morgue.

"Where's she going?" Levi asked.

"Only one way to find out," Sasha answered as the two, holding Stan between them, followed their friend out into the hallway.

With Levi's flashlight illuminating the way, they watched as Addison, with her hand awkwardly outstretched, walked down the darkened corridor. Wondering where she was going, they received their answer when she slipped into a room at the end of the passage.

"This is getting spookier by the minute," Levi muttered under his breath as they reluctantly tried to keep up with her.

"This whole night has been nothing but spooky," Sasha replied. "I give you permission to rip me a new one if I ever come up with any more cockamamie ideas on getting famous."

Levi inwardly laughed. Knowing Sasha's volatile Latina temper, he'd only get two words out before she'd unleash hell upon his head. But he'd file away her vow just in case.

"I think one of us should stay out in the hallway and keep an eye out for Devon," Stan replied as they reached the doorway Addison had disappeared into. "There's no sense the four of us getting trapped in there."

Sasha and Levi shivered. The last thing they needed was to be locked up in the eerie basement, at the mercy of the Monster of the Asylum and whatever else was haunting this building. Considering how desperate Devon would be to keep secret what he'd tried to do to Stan, they wouldn't put it past him to lock them inside the room and throw away the key. And once the crew left the asylum, how long would it be before they were found? Or in what condition they'd be in if and when they were discovered?

"Great idea," Sasha said. "Levi, you stand guard."

"I was thinking I'd like to be the one to keep watch," Stan replied. "I owe the shit for conking me over the head and stuffing me into one of the morgue cells."

"You're in no condition to put up much of a fight, bro," she replied.

He disentangled himself from his friends and stood upright. "See? I'm feeling better."

"You still look like shit. Tell you what. If Levi has to knock him out, we'll let you spit on him as we step over his body. How's that?"

"I suppose it will have to do."

At first Addison had no idea where the little girl had led her to. But she immediately felt a sense of dread. The room reeked of evil, of deeds done here in secret that she wasn't sure she wanted to see. Yet, even without words, she felt the little girl's persistence. Whatever occurred in this room, it was important to the girl that Addison witness it.

The world needs to know.

Addison jumped. She looked down at the girl, but instead of looking up at her, the youngster's attention was on what looked like a giant furnace taking up one wall of the room.

Why are you showing me this? I don't understand.

Her only response was the girl pointing urgently at the furnace. Addison had no choice but to look to where the girl indicated.

It took her a few moments to realize that the room was changing. The decrepit abandoned surroundings were slowly morphing into an area that appeared to be cared for. The walls were no longer peeling, nor was there dust and cobwebs littering the ceilings. Her blood froze when she heard an eerily familiar song playing over an old-fashioned radio propped up on a shelf on the other side of the room.

It was Stairway to Heaven by Led Zeppelin.

A gurney appeared in front of her on which a motionless body was strapped.

Addison felt sick to her stomach when she realized it was the lifeless body of the girl now holding her hand. She wanted to turn away, to stop the motion picture playing before her, but she couldn't move. She was frozen in place, whether by the girl or by something else, she couldn't tell. All she knew was that she *needed* to see what was about to happen.

Addison gasped aloud as she saw a man in an orderly's uniform appear out of the darkness. His face was bathed in shadows as he opened the doors to the furnace. She immediately found herself immersed in unbearable heat as the flames licked at the opening. He walked to the front of the gurney and ran his hands lovingly over the girl's bare feet. The sight of him caressing the youngster's skin sent a disgusted shiver up Addison's spine.

What was he doing? Why was she being forced to witness this?

She sucked in her breath when he abruptly tipped the table

up and the tiny body slid into the flames.

Oh God, no! Addison screamed in her mind as the girl disappeared into the fire.

To her horror, the man's face, illuminated by the flames, turned slowly and looked directly at her.

And smiled.

It was the man from her nightmare! The man who had terrorized her since she'd arrived at Meadowlark.

She suddenly remembered the journal Sasha had found. The memory of what she'd read flooded in. Dr. Fisher writing about the disappearance of a twelve year old girl. An orderly finding human remains in the furnace room. The riot.

She's making me see the truth of what happened to her. To what happened to all of them. She needs me to know that Gerald Harper is the Monster of the Asylum. And now he knows I'm here. And that I know his secret.

Her terror grew as he suddenly launched himself at her. Addison screamed and ran, only to crash against Stan and Sasha. Together, the three of them tumbled onto the floor.

"Oh God, oh God," she sobbed as she desperately tried to untangle herself from her friends' limbs. "He's going to kill me. I have to get out of here!"

"Addy, calm down!" Sasha cried out as she barely missed being punched by a hysterical Addison as she fought to get to her feet and escape this nightmare. It was Stan who finally grabbed Addison by the shoulders, and gave her a hard shake.

"Addison, you're alright!" he shouted in her face. "There's no one here."

"No, no, no. I know what he did. He's going to kill me to keep me quiet."

"That's what he wants you to think. You're safe. I swear it."

Somehow Stan's words penetrated her panic. She blinked at him several times. Then, as if she recognized him for the first time, she fell into his arms. Stunned that the girl of his dreams was sobbing against his chest, he held her closer to him, luxuriating in the feel of her hair against his cheek even as he realized they had no time for this. It was imperative they get out of there.

"You're sitting on my leg," Sasha complained as she pushed against Stan. "Move before you cut off my circulation."

The spell was broken. Inwardly cursing Sasha for her terrible sense of timing, he reluctantly let Addison go.

"Are you okay now?" he asked as he looked into her tear stained face.

"I won't be okay until we're miles from here."

They scrambled to their feet and met up with Levi in the corridor.

"So far I don't hear anything, but we need to make tracks," he replied.

The four hurried to the staircase and held their breaths as they ascended them as quietly as they could. Coming onto the ground floor and knowing basecamp was nearby, they snuck to the front door, shocked to see it standing wide open.

"Maybe someone else got smart and decided to get out of Dodge while they still could," Sasha whispered as they tore down the stairs and out into the cold night.

The moonlight shone around them, illuminating the grounds and sending off shadows that now looked menacing. Addison uttered a strangled cry when she felt something squishy under her boot.

"Shhhh!" Sasha reprimanded her. "We can't let Devon know we're out here."

"I'm sorry, but I forgot about the dead crows," she said as she shivered in disgust.

"Crap, is it my imagination or are there more dead birds now?" Levi asked. The four looked about them and saw Levi was right. The ground was now littered with at least a hundred dead black carcasses.

"Another reason to put as much distance between us and this place," Sasha replied grimly.

The four huddled together as they walked gingerly among the deceased crows. Levi started towards the first van only to have Sasha abruptly pull him back.

"We need to go to the last van. It's under the shadows of the trees and not as visible from the front door."

"You sound like you've done this before," he said, staring at her in awe.

"Some things are better left unsaid," she answered cryptically.

They reached the van and Levi let out a curse when they found the doors were locked. He and Sasha hurried to the other vans, but found they too were locked.

"Shit, shit, shit," Levi muttered in anger when they reunited with Addison and Stan. "I was sure they'd left the keys in the ignition. I mean, for chrissakes, who's crazy enough to come out here to steal a bunch of vans?"

"Those must be the keys I saw Brandon place on the table next to the monitors," Stan replied. "How are we going to get them without giving away what we're planning to do?"

"We need a diversion," Sasha replied. She turned to Addison. "You're the most innocent-looking one in the group."

Addison raised an eyebrow. "I'm not sure that's a compliment."

"Trust me, it's a good thing. I'll hide in the hallway. You create the diversion to lure Brandon out of there. When he's gone, I'll slip in, grab the keys and voila! Instant escape."

"I'm not going back into that building," she replied adamantly.

Sasha reached out and laid her hand on Addison's shoulder. "I'm sorry, Addy, but you have to. It's the only way we're going to get out of here."

"Why don't you do it?"

"Because I'm not as believable as you are."

"And how am I supposed to divert him?"

They fell silent as they tried to figure out the best way to entice Brandon to leave basecamp.

Finally Levi said, "If he's anything like the others, his end all and be all is ratings. Since you're the psychic, what if you tell him you found something he needs to see?"

"He could just say he'd rather see it on the monitors," she pointed out.

"Listen, I might be wrong, but I sat next to the dude for hours and I never got the sense he was a dick like Devon," Stan replied. "I mean, yeah, he probably knew about the set-ups, but I really don't think he would actually hurt anyone to keep them from spilling the beans about all the fakery."

"So?" Sasha asked.

"So, what if Addison tells him she found me, but she needs help getting me to safety? Maybe I fell down a hole and she can't lift me up?"

"That's a big 'if,' Stan," Levi said. "We don't know how deeply involved he is in all of this. And what about Mark or Tina or any of the cameramen? What if they're all at basecamp when Addison goes in?"

"Actually, that could work to our advantage," Sasha spoke up. "If there are enough people in the room, and she says she found you, that's bound to cause a ruckus. While they're running around, Addy can grab the keys without anyone noticing." She looked to each of her friends. "We really don't have any other options."

Addison shivered. The memory of the Monster's face smiling at her was still vivid. Too close for comfort. She knew they needed to leave, and she desperately wanted to help. But she didn't think she had it in her to go back into that building.

Seeing her distress, Levi threw his arm around her shoulders. "I'll go in there with you. I'll stand right by the door that leads to basecamp. Any sign of trouble and I'll whisk you out of there before you know it."

With her friends looking at her, depending on her, Addison had no choice but to reluctantly agree. Taking Levi's hand, the two warily made their way back over the carpet of dead birds before re-entering the asylum.

Levi hid in the shadows near the door while Addison took a deep breath and let it out slowly. Throwing back her shoulders, she entered basecamp.

She found Reggie, Todd and Brandon gathered around one of the monitors. To her relief, Devon wasn't present. The three were so intent on whatever they were watching, they didn't notice her at first. Which she used to her advantage. She took a few steps back, then dashed into the room, making sure to stand next to the table where she saw the van keys laid out.

"Oh my God!" she yelled. "I found Stan! He's badly hurt. I need your help."

"Where is he?" Todd asked, whirling around towards her.

"He's up on the third floor," she lied. "He fell through a broken floorboard in one of the rooms. We tried to call for an ambulance, but our phones are dead. Please hurry! He's covered in blood."

She pretended to burst into sobs, praying they wouldn't notice there were no tears on her face. Just as she'd hoped, pandemonium broke out as Reggie and Todd hurried to gather first aid kits and rope in order to pull Stan out from the floor.

With Brandon's back to her and trying to be as inconspicuous as possible, she reached behind, swooped up the first pair of keys her fingers touched on, and shoved them into her back pocket.

"Where exactly is he?" Todd asked.

"He's up near the rec room. Sasha and Levi are there, trying their best to keep him calm."

Realizing they might ask her to accompany them, and thinking fast, she fell back onto one of the chairs and began to cry hysterically. Just as she'd hoped, they saw she was too distraught to move so they left without her.

"Brandon, you call for an ambulance," Todd instructed as he and Reggie dashed off.

As Brandon reached for the walkie-talkie, Addison seized the opportunity and slipped out of the room.

Coming out from the shadows where he'd been hiding, she and Levi shared a palm slap before running outside.

Reaching Sasha and Stan, Addison pushed the unlock button on the key. They heard a beep as the lights blinked on a van two vehicles down from where they stood.

Hurrying towards the van, the wind suddenly came up and slammed against them, almost hurtling them to the ground. As they struggled against the gale, Addison heard what sounded like human whispers laced within the gust itself. She couldn't make out what the words were, but it sent a shiver of fear through her.

Just as quickly as it started, the wind abruptly died down. Scrambling towards the van, they all stopped as the sounds of fluttering caught everyone's attention. It grew louder, interspersed with whirlpools of leaves blowing up into the air, until it threatened to overwhelm the teenagers.

"What is that?' Sasha demanded as she looked up at the sky.

Once again, the wind blew up. The whispers grew louder. The fluttering noises increased in volume.

Without warning, Stan stopped and pointed at the ground. "Holy shit!" he yelled. "Look!"

To their horror, they watched as the crows they'd believed were dead, begin to rustle their feathers and sit up. Suddenly, as if in sync with each other, a cloud of black birds rose up into the air and fluttered above them.

Their fascination at what they were seeing suddenly turned to panic when the birds turned.

And headed straight for them.

"Quick! Get into the van!" Levi screamed as they threw themselves at the vehicle.

They were just closing the doors behind them when the birds hurled themselves against the windows.

"Hurry! Get us out of here!" Addison yelled as Sasha threw the vehicle into drive and barreled out of the parking area.

The birds continued to launch themselves against the windshield, causing Sasha to curse aloud as she tried to keep the vehicle on the road.

"I can't believe this shit!" she cried out as she barely managed to keep from swerving the steering wheel to avoid the crows. "They were dead! I know they were dead."

"This entire area appears to be stuck in some sort of vortex where the rules of gravity, relativity and time don't exist," Stan spoke up.

"Ya think?" Sasha retorted, flinching as a particularly large bird crashed against the windshield, creating a hairline crack along the glass. "I don't know how much longer the windshield is going to hold," she warned as several cracks began to appear.

Looking out the side window, Addison's heart skidded to a stop. Emerging from the surrounding forest were what looked like people. They were all dressed in hospital gowns and were quickly converging on the road they needed to drive down to leave the grounds of the asylum.

"Hurry!" Addison urged Sasha. "They're coming."

"Who's coming? Who are you talking about?"

The car was suddenly filled with the din of whispers. Levi and Stan covered their ears with their hands, while Sasha looked into the rearview mirror at Addison.

"What the hell is that? What are they saying?"

Addison looked up and met Sasha's eye reflected back at her. "They're the old patients."

"That's crazy! They've been dead for years."

"As dead as the crows were?"

Sasha had no response to that.

The whispering grew louder until Sasha wanted to scream. She turned her head and instantly caught her breath when she saw more patients emerging from the woods and heading towards the road. "I don't believe this," she whispered under her breath. "This cannot be happening."

She turned her gaze back out the cracked windshield. Suddenly, without warning, she slammed on the brakes, sending Levi into the dashboard, while Addison and Stan smashed against the back of the front seats.

"*¡Mierda!*" Sasha yelled out in Spanish, as the van skidded to a stop.

"Are you crazy? Why the hell did you—" Levi started to yell, only to have the words shrivel in his throat.

"We can't stop now, Sasha! We have to keep going," Stan shouted.

When there was no response, he pulled himself up from the floor when he'd landed. Frantic that they were about to be attacked by God knows what, and upset she'd stopped their only means of escape, he started to protest when he looked out the windshield.

"Jesus," Stan muttered under his breath.

The four watched in horror as a figure staggered in the middle of the road, trying to make its way towards them. Its face was covered in blood and its clothes hung in tattered shreds. One arm was outstretched towards the van as if begging for help.

"Dear God," Sasha whispered. "It's a damned zombie."

CHAPTER FOURTEEN

"I'll show them," Devon muttered under his breath as he ascended the third floor steps. Tucked under his arm was the spare video camera and tripod.

When the location was finally chosen, Devon had gone out on a preliminary trip to scope out potential areas to set up, not only the technical equipment, but his 'ghost tricks'. His guide, a representative from Ashboro, refused to enter the building, a situation that suited him perfectly.

As he'd walked around the location, ideas flooded in on where best to place his set-ups. He thought to make the grand finale up in the attic where Jurgen Knowles had fallen to his death. Finding a photograph of the doomed investigator on the internet, he couldn't think of a better place to set up that image, in the form of a ghostly apparition, than where the man had died. However, when he reached the attic, he almost lost his own life when his foot went through a floorboard. Thankfully, he'd been able to pull himself back before he plunged to the floor below. That's when he reluctantly came to the conclusion that the attic was much too dangerous, even for him. He would need to find another place to set up the hologram of Jurgen's ghost.

He finally settled on what had once been a conference room. It was one of the more decrepit rooms he'd come across, and it lent the perfect air of eeriness to pull off the trick.

Now as he made his way toward the site of his grand finale, he congratulated himself on setting the trick up. It had taken him longer than he'd thought, but it was his ace in the hole. With the investigation slipping out of his control, he needed this. The show needed this.

This trick is guaranteed to bring the ratings up. And when they do, Mark and Tina are history. No one shows disloyalty to me and gets away with it. Screw 'em both.

Smiling at the thought of how much this episode was going to catapult him back to the top of the ratings, he suddenly heard the stairs creak behind him..

Although he'd been careful to slip away without anyone noticing him, he paused to make sure he hadn't been followed. He needed to be alone. His plan counted on it.

When he saw no one on the stair, he let out a sigh of relief. So far, so good.

Yet, as he continued up to the conference room, he couldn't help but wonder what had caused the steps to creak. They'd been going up and down the stairs all evening and they only squeaked when someone put their weight on them.

Ah well, whatever. I've got too much to worry about than whether a century's old stair creaks or not.

He chided himself for his sudden lack of focus. He'd need all of his fortitude if he was going to pull this off.

He thought back to the early days when he, Mark and Brandon had first started The Ghost Dudes. Back then, they'd genuinely set out to prove the existence of life after death. Yet, once the show fell in their laps, it quickly became evident that what the audience craved wasn't scientific proof as much as thrills and chills. They loved being scared. Unfortunately, spirits didn't always cooperate. Investigating the paranormal took patience. It could take hours and hours before even the most menial of ghostly activity could be captured. But with the average attention span growing ever shorter, The Ghost Dudes needed to provide the wow factor if they hoped to survive.

Devon was willing to do whatever it took to stay on the air. If the audience wanted to be scared, he'd scare them whether it was real or manufactured. And tonight, on All Hallow's Eve, Devon was about to provide them with a specter so terrifying and menacing, they'd be talking about it for years to come.

***

"You can't stop!" Levi cried out. "You've got to keep going!"

The headlights of the van cut a path through the dark night, illuminating the figure before them. Blood covered the left side of its face as it shuffled closer towards them. Wild eyes stared back through strands of hair matted with dry leaves and muck.

"That thing doesn't look like the others," Sasha whispered. "It's solid." She leaned forward in her seat and peered through the cracked windshield. "I think it's real."

Levi followed her gaze. Suddenly, he gasped out loud.

"Holy shit!" he cried.

Before anyone could stop him, he opened the van door and jumped out.

"Levi! What are you doing? Get back here!" Stan screamed. To his shock, Addison now opened the van door and also jumped out. "What is going on here? Has everyone gone crazy?"

"Stan, open your door," Sasha ordered.

"Are you insane? No friggin' way."

"Open the door, you idiot. That's not a ghost out there. It's Tina!"

Stan pushed himself forward and watched in horror as Tina suddenly collapsed to the ground. Levi swiftly swooped her up in his arms as he and Addison hurried back to the van.

"Open the damned door!" Sasha yelled.

Jarred by her outburst, Stan slid open the door just as Levi came up. Pushed towards the opposite window, he watched as

Addison jumped in and helped Levi place the semi-conscious woman on the bench seat.

"Drive!" Levi ordered as he slid back into the front seat.

Addison shifted her weight and leaned towards Tina. "What happened to you?" she asked.

Tina lifted her face and stared blankly at Addison. She mumbled incoherently. The teenager's heart stopped. Devon had mentioned that previous investigators had never been the same after visiting Meadowlark.

Had the asylum claimed another victim?

Sasha turned away from Tina and looked out the windshield. "You've got to be friggin' kidding me."

Everyone followed Sasha's stare.

Through the torrent of dried leaves whipping furiously about the van, Addison caught sight of the subject of Sasha's distress. Her scream caught in her throat as she watched hundreds of semi-transparent patients standing in the middle of the road, blocking their escape.

"How is this happening?" the Latina whispered under her breath.

"This house eats souls."

The four turned to stare at Tina who abruptly sat up. The disheveled woman looked to each of them, before her eyes glazed over and she slid back against the seat.

"That works for me," Sasha said. Smashing the shift into drive, she closed her eyes, punched the gas and drove straight through them.

***

"There have been reports of a ghost seen walking into what was once the conference room. This is what we refer to as a residual haunting. It's nothing more than an imprint in time. A scar if you will. A scar that repeats itself over and over."

Devon adjusted the GoPro camera strapped around his forehead to give the audience a better view of the hallway. "An interactive haunting is just what the term implies. It's when a ghost interacts with the living. Those who are sensitive to energy will tell you that the way to tell the difference between a residual haunting and an interactive haunting is that a residual haunting will have no human emotion or energy tied to it. It really is like watching a movie replay itself constantly. An interactive haunting, on the other hand…" The words died in his throat when he suddenly felt the temperature plunge. To his surprise he saw his breath vaporize before him. "Holy cow, hopefully you can see this." He blew out his breath again and watched the mist rise up in the air. "The temperature has just gone down by at least twenty degrees. And we all know what that means!"

He took a few steps toward the conference room and jerked to a halt. He blinked several times to make sure he wasn't seeing things. He hadn't activated the fake ghost image, yet standing in front of him was the figure of a man. He was dressed in an orderly's uniform, the front of which was stained with blood.

His excitement grew. Was it possible? Was he seeing the same ghost Addison had seen? Or were Mark and Tina playing another trick?

"Welcome, Devon. I've been waiting for you."

This was new. In all the ghost tricks he'd ever pulled, he'd never been able to figure out a way to have an apparition conduct a conversation with him. If he couldn't do it, there was no way Mark or Tina could ever do it either.

Shit! I'm speaking with an honest-to-God ghost.

"Who are you?" Devon asked.

His exhilaration increased when he noticed he was looking *through* the figure standing before him. Afraid to look away, he could only hope his camera was capturing all of this.

His grand finale was going to be better than he could have

ever hoped for or dreamed of.

"I run this asylum. You're here because I've allowed it."

Devon let out a nervous laugh. "Is that right?" he asked in false bravado. He abruptly felt the air grow heavy, as if his words had angered the spirit.

The ghost raised his hand and pointed it at Devon.

Oh shit.

***

Brandon watched the monitor in growing panic. He'd tried to call the ambulance, only to discover his phone was dead. He tried several times to rouse the others on the walkie-talkie, but he was getting no response. Desperate to discover if they'd found Stan, he was about to leave basecamp when he caught the figure of Devon on the monitor. There was something about the image that made him pause. He turned up the audio and frowned. What the hell was Devon up to? The man was standing in the corridor talking to himself.

Unable to fathom what Devon was doing, Brandon grabbed the remote and zoomed the hallway camera in toward the part of the corridor that Devon was focused on.

He saw nothing.

He wasn't sure what game Devon was playing, and it made him nervous. The audience was seeing what he was seeing. And to all extent and purposes, it looked as though Devon had lost his mind.

***

"I know why you're here."

"Oh yeah," Devon responded. "Why is that?"

"You want what everyone wants. You want to be famous."

"I already am famous."

The hallway echoed with a harsh laugh that sent a chill

down Devon's spine.

"There are two types of fame, my friend. There is the fame that lasts a lifetime."

"Nothing wrong with that."

"Oh really? Tell me Devon, would you like to be remembered like Jack Benny?"

"Who's that?"

"Exactly. Then there's the fame that lasts *forever*. Think of Julius Caesar. Surely you've heard of him."

"Of course. Who hasn't heard of Caesar?"

The spirit chuckled. "Two thousand years after his death and we still speak of him."

"Okay, I see what you mean. That's pretty much a no-brainer."

"I thought you would say that. Follow me, Devon Watson and become immortal. Achieve the fame that will keep your name on the public's lips forever."

The ghost disappeared, only to reappear at the other end of the hallway. He beckoned the investigator with his finger.

Devon hesitated. He now knew this wasn't a trick conjured up by Mark or Tina. This was the real deal. And he had a pretty good idea who he was speaking to. Should he trust a creature who was considered the embodiment of evil? Yet even as he thought this, he couldn't risk jeopardizing what he was capturing on film. The image of the Monster of the Asylum would make him millions. And catapult his name into the rarified realm of true immortality.

He had no choice. He had to follow.

*** *** ***

Brandon watched as Devon turned and walked back down the corridor. Expecting him to return to basecamp, he was horrified when Devon walked up the stairs towards the attic. The one place they were forbidden to enter.

"Devon, what are you doing!" he shouted at the monitor. "Have you totally lost it?"

Suddenly the picture was gone, replaced by a loud static. Then the screen went dead.

***

Devon reached the entrance to the attic. Part of him knew how dangerous it was to be up here. But he couldn't risk losing what he was filming. It was too important, too monumental to stop.

LED flashlight in hand, he aimed the beam in front of him. He was astonished to find that the police tape that had cordoned off this area was no longer in place. And the floor was now fully intact. The hole he'd seen when he'd first come up here months before was gone.

Taking a step further into the attic, he swung the light back and forth and was further amazed to see how much the attic had been cleaned up. Unlike the rest of the asylum, there were no cobwebs, falling plaster or broken floorboards. For whatever reason, the state authorities had come in and refurbished the attic. So why were they so adamant that no one come up here? Was it because they considered this room some sort of macabre memorial to the German investigator who had lost his life here?

"Yes, this room was repaired just for you. You see, you and I are very much alike," the voice said, beckoning him forward. "We both stop at nothing to achieve greatness. We allow no one to stand in our way."

Devon nodded. He couldn't get over how the ghost was able to mine his very soul to uncover the person Devon truly was.

He's the only one who understands me.

"Set up your camera so the world can witness your greatness."

Devon removed the GoPro and strapped it to the railing.

"Wonderful, Devon. Now, come closer so I can show you what your new life will be like. Tell me again what it is you want?"

"I want to be immortal," Devon whispered.

"Perfect. And so you shall be."

He reached out his hand to Devon. Who stepped forward to take it.

***

"Devon, do you read me? Come in, dammit." Brandon was met by static. He threw the walkie talkie down in disgust.

Todd and Reggie entered basecamp, followed by Mark.

"I don't know what that girl was talking about. We didn't find any sign of Stan anywhere," Todd replied.

"Forget Stan," Brandon spoke up. "I've lost all communication with Devon. We need to find him."

"He's probably rigging up another one of his ghostly adventures," Todd chuckled.

Brandon threw him worried look. "You don't understand. Just before I lost the feed, he was talking to himself."

"So what?"

"He was on his way to the attic."

"That's impossible," Mark scoffed. "He knows better than to go up there."

"Take a look for yourself then, if you don't believe me."

Brandon rewound the tape and the three men watched in mounting unease as the image of Devon having a one sided conversation played back.

Mark audibly gasped when he saw his friend mount the stairs toward the attic. "That makes absolutely no sense."

"Whether it does or it doesn't, we have to find him," Brandon repeated. "Reggie, Todd, grab the walkie talkies and try to round up Tina and the kids. Mark and I will go after Devon."

The two men took the stairs three at a time. Rounding the landing, they slowed their step and proceeded cautiously towards the attic.

"Why would Devon do this? We were nearing the grand finale that was going to end this investigation with a huge ratings bonanza," Brandon said as they gingerly put their weight on each step to ensure the floor would support them.

"I don't know," Mark replied shortly.

Brandon stopped and glanced at him. "What aren't you saying? I can tell by the tone of your voice there's more to this."

Mark paused, then let out a breath. "We had a bit of an argument. He's been acting more egotistical than usual."

"I noticed that. He threatened to fire me."

"I think he threatened to fire all of us."

"But is that enough to make him jeopardize *everything?*"

Mark had no answer.

As they continued up the darkened stairs, dust filled the air. It wasn't long before the two men began coughing.

"Look. You can see his footprints in the dust," Brandon pointed out.

Mark nodded. He was already scared, but the sight of the footprints sent a chill down his spine.

Why are you doing this, Devon? What in God's name is up here that would make you risk your life?

The temperature grew colder as they climbed up each step. Wooden slats, chunks of old newspaper and pieces of insulation hung out of various holes in the wall. The cracking of plaster under their boots accompanied the creaking of the stairs.

As the two men reached the top of the landing, they ducked under the police tape. It was then they noticed a red light shining in the darkness. Brandon turned his flashlight towards it.

"Isn't that one of our GoPro cameras?" Mark asked.

"What's it doing tied to the railing?"

"Devon grabbed one before he came up here."

"Oh shit," Mark muttered under his breath.

Brandon reached out and grabbed the GoPro. They withdrew back to the landing where he pressed a button on the LCD screen. A moment later, a video began to play. They saw the picture jiggle up and down as the person they assumed to be Devon climbed the stairs they'd just come up. Along the way, they heard him having the same one-sided conversation they'd seen him having in the hallway. Listening to his words, their blood chilled.

They watched the camera capture the dilapidated attic before the images jerked and Devon's hands came into view.

"This must be when he's tying the camera to the railing," Mark replied.

They watched the images settle down as the lens now pointed towards the center of the attic.

Both men caught their breath as they saw the hole in the center of the floor for the first time.

Devon's image abruptly came into view and he said a few words.

"Wait. What did he say? I couldn't hear that," Mark replied.

Brandon hit the volume and raised it as high as it could go. He then hit rewind and stopped at the spot where Devon first appeared. He hit play.

"I want to be immortal," Devon said.

Their hearts stopped as they watched Devon step forward without hesitation or fear.

They could do nothing but watch helplessly and incomprehensively as their friend and colleague walked towards the hole as if it wasn't there. A moment later, he disappeared as he fell straight down through the floor.

"Christ, no!" Brandon yelled out.

The two men turned on their heels and hurried down to the

floor below. Turning at the landing, they ran down the corridor, quickly looking in each room.

"Devon! Answer us! Devon!" Mark called in a panic. "Where are you?"

Brandon, who was several feet ahead of Mark, opened a door and shone his flashlight inside. A moment later he uttered a cry and disappeared into the room.

Mark came up and hesitated. The rusted placard on the wall indicated this was the chapel.

He was terrified to enter. He wasn't sure he wanted to see what had happened to Devon.

He's your friend. You have to go in there.

With limbs shaking, Mark swung open the door and shone his flashlight. He caught sight of Brandon standing several feet from the altar. His face was contorted into a look of horror that chilled Mark's blood.

Forcing himself forward, he walked up to Brandon and stood beside him. The technician lifted his hand, rested it on Mark's shoulder and gently pushed him in the direction of the altar.

With his heart pounding in his chest, Mark turned and with shaking hands, raised his flashlight.

"Oh God, no!" he screamed as he fell to his knees.

Devon's body hung in front of the altar, his face frozen in a soundless scream. His eyes stared lifelessly up at the religious murals painted on the ceiling while blood saturated his shirt from the cast iron rod impaled through his chest.

Above his head, written in blood on the wall were the words, *I'm immortal.*

EPILOGUE

PRESS RELEASE
NOVEMBER 2, 2018

LOS ANGELES. The families of Addison Monroe, Sasha Marquez, Stanley Crane and Levi Taylor express their deep sorrow and regret over the untimely and tragic loss of Devon Watson. The four, members of a Massachusetts paranormal investigation team known as The Ghost Seekers, were chosen from thousands of entries to participate in a live investigation of the Meadowlark Mental Asylum, broadcast last Halloween, with the hosts of the popular The Ghost Dudes.

"He was very concerned over our safety throughout the entire investigation," Sasha Marquez announced through their spokes-person. "He made sure to tell us never to go up into the attic because of the unsafe floor-boards." When asked if they cared to speculate why Watson defied his own warnings and went up into the unsafe attic, the four teenagers could offer no explanation. "It's as much a mystery to us as it is to everyone else," Levi Taylor said.

The Massachusetts State Medical Examiner's office has ruled Watson's death an accident. In an effort to prevent another such tragedy from occurring, Mayor Charles Lintner of Ashboro, Massachusetts, the town where Meadowlark is located, has introduced legislation to have the asylum, built in 1867, torn down. Preservation activists have protested his decision, citing the example of the Danvers State Mental Hospital, also located in Massachusetts. Rather than tear down the historic building, Danvers was converted into condominiums. The activists are hoping the same can be done with Meadowlark.

Fans have speculated whether the popular television program will return without the leader-ship of the charismatic Watson. The network has yet to decide.

Three weeks later

They'd gathered at the gazebo in Radley Park. It was the first time the friends were meeting after the Halloween tragedy. After seeing firsthand the dark side of fame - the endless rumors and speculation about what really happened at the Meadowlark Asylum and the part they'd played in Devon's death, they were more than ready to bury themselves back in Millbrook. But not before enduring endless meetings with the network attorneys and publicity department who pressed them to reveal what happened.

Addison decided it was best not to talk about her personal experiences with The Monster of the Asylum. She was pretty sure the 'men in suits' would never understand, much less believe, what she and her friends had seen. The others followed suit. Before her camera could be confiscated, Sasha quickly downloaded the photograph of the ghost with no eyes onto a thumb drive and hid it in her bra. When Stan mentioned the fakery he'd discovered and how Devon had knocked him out and placed him in the morgue cell, the suits quickly came back with a settlement of cash, and an insistence they all sign a non-disclosure agreement, forbidding them from ever speaking publicly about what happened inside the asylum. Since they'd already decided to keep quiet, they signed the agreement, took their money and buried themselves back in Millbrook.

They thought it best to lay low, not only to recover from the disaster, but to keep from being a target of the paparazzi who swarmed into the small town in the hopes of snaring an interview with the teenagers. The fact that Levi's father was the police chief went a long way towards keeping the press off their backs. He spoke to the high school and the four were allowed to study at home for the fall semester. It was hoped when they returned to class in January, the furor would have died down.

After two weeks of failing to see, much less talk to the four, the press finally left town. The friends waited one more week to make sure they were safe before deciding to regroup at their usual meeting spot, the gazebo in Radley Park.

"Fame sucks," Sasha said when she swung up into the gazebo and threw herself down next to Levi. "I thought I'd go stark raving mad if I had to spend one more day holed up in my house."

"Tell me about it," Levi concurred. "I was beginning to feel like a vampire. Stay indoors during the day and sneak out in the yard at night just to get a breath of fresh air. And only after letting Chomley out to make sure there weren't any reporters hiding in the bushes." He smiled. "Chomley hates strangers."

"Chomley hates everyone," Sasha retorted, referring to the Taylor family bulldog, who'd gone after her ankles more times than she cared to remember.

"I still can't believe Devon is dead," she continued as she nervously flicked at the zipper on her jacket. "And Tina being…well…never quite the same again. I know it's been a few weeks, but I still can't wrap my head around it."

"No matter how many times I go over it, I can't figure out why he went upstairs," Levi said, echoing their sentiments. "He knew how dangerous it was up there."

"You're going to want to see this then," Sasha said as she took her phone out. "I was surfing YouTube when I found this video. I'm guessing it was leaked after the news hit that Devon had died."

The friends gathered around as Sasha pulled up a video and hit play. They saw a young, slightly heavy man walking up the stairs to the attic in the Meadowlark Asylum. He was speaking in German, but someone had put the translation on the bottom of the screen.

"Of course I want to be immortal. Who wouldn't want to be immortal?" Stan read from the translation.

"Shit," Levi muttered, his eyes wide with astonishment.

"I didn't say anything to you guys, but when we were at the network offices, I overheard Mark and Brandon talking. They were discussing the GoPro video that Devon recorded." Sasha's dark eyes took in her friends. "Devon did the exact same thing this German guy did. He walked up the stairs to the attic, talking to himself about being immortal."

"That is so insane," Levi replied.

"He isn't talking to himself," Addison said. "I know it sounds crazy, but the Monster of the Asylum had something to do with both deaths. I'm not sure why yet, but it's as clear to me as it is sitting here with you guys."

"Are you saying you think the Monster lured them up to their deaths?" Levi asked incredulously.

"That's exactly what I'm saying."

They continued to watch as Jurgen came up the landing and started across the attic floor. Sasha reached out and quickly stopped the video.

"You don't want to see the rest of this," she said grimly.

"Because he falls through the floor like Devon did?" Levi asked.

She nodded.

"But why kill them that way?" Levi asked. "What's so significant about the way they died?"

"Maybe this will answer our question." Sasha reached into her jacket pocket and withdrew the rolled-up journal.

"What are you doing with that?" Addison asked, aghast at the sight of it. "We were supposed to turn over everything we found to the network."

Sasha shrugged. "I forgot." Seeing Addison's disbelieving look, she threw up her hands. "Okay, okay, so I deliberately forgot. But you can't blame me. From day one we were kept completely in the dark – not only about what really happened back on October 31, 1975, but what caused the Monster of the Asylum to make that building his home. It's pretty obvious there was some kind of cover-up. If they could do it once, they could do it again." Her voice lowered to a whisper. "Something bad happened there. We saw the ghosts of the patients. We heard their cries for help."

The four fell into an uneasy silence.

"I've spent the last few weeks trying to make sense of it all," Stan said, breaking the stillness. "I've been on the internet for hours researching ghosts – why they exist. Why they remain on the earth plane. Why they don't move on. It's my conclusion that what we saw and experienced were clues."

"Clues?" Levi asked dubiously.

"Yes. Some souls remain trapped because they need the truth to get out. They need the living to validate that they were once human beings who lived and breathed, who loved, who suffered. Who once walked this earth. They need their stories to be revealed so they can come to some kind of closure." He picked up the journal and held it in his hand. "There's a reason Sasha found this journal. It may be our only way of putting together the clues the dead gave us. We owe it to them to stop the cover-up and unravel the secrets of Meadowlark Asylum once and for all."

"I don't see how this journal is going to help. Addison read the last entry when she found it," Sasha pointed out.

Stan's face fell in disappointment. He'd been certain the answers to what happened to them were in the journal. He was about to put it back when he paused. Instead, he idly flipped through it.

"It says here the journal belonged to Dr. Joseph Fisher."

"Todd said he was the administrator of the Meadowlark Asylum," Sasha answered.

"Is he still alive?" Stan asked.

She turned to her phone and looked up the doctor on the internet. Her eyes darted back and forth as she read the screen. "It just says he died in 1975." She suddenly shivered. "According to what Addison read, Fisher was hiding in his office while the patients rioted outside. God, they must have gotten inside."

"Do you think the patients killed him?" Levi whispered.

Sasha shrugged.

"Hey, wait a minute," Stan exclaimed. "There's an entry in the back of the journal." He put the notebook back on the table and the three huddled over his shoulder. "Look at the writing at the front of the journal."

"He's talking about a couple of his patients," Levi said as he quickly scanned the neatly spaced words.

"I mean, look at the handwriting. It looks like the kind of handwriting you'd do at the end of the day when you have some time on your hands."

"What's your point?" Sasha asked.

"Now look at the entry I found." He flipped the journal to the rear and showed it to them.

"Wow. It's barely legible," Addison said.

"Exactly. It's obvious he was trying his best to get the words down before—"

Stan didn't need to say it for the friends to know what he was referring to.

"Can you read it?" Sasha questioned.

"I can try."

He leaned over the journal and began to slowly read it aloud, stumbling here and there over words that were hard to decipher.

I need to get these words written. They may very well be the last words I ever write and I need the world to understand what happened here. I'm just not sure I comprehend it myself. I've spent my life looking after the forgotten of humanity. But to see first hand what humans are capable of...

The horror is indescribable. The patients have become no better than animals. No, not animals. Worse. I've just witnessed the orderly Gerald Harper being set upon by a mob of patients. They are screaming for vengeance. For revenge for all he's done to them. They're beneath my window and oh my God, they are impaling him with a wooden stake through the chest! I can't believe it.

Yet I must. My heart breaks. I realize now I share the blame. I allowed it all to come to this horrific end. Patients disappearing without a trace. His insistence they ran away. Did I trust the wrong man? Was I too willing to listen to him because I didn't want to face the truth?

I hear the sirens. The police are on their way. Thank God, thank God. There's a chance I may be saved. Please hurry! They need to stop the mutilation of Gerald's body.

Dear God, no! The patients are at my door. It's locked but they're determined to get at me. They blame me for everything. I should have been more vigilant. They won't listen to me. The door frame is breaking. I must hide this journal and pray it gets found.

I must pray for my life. For my soul.

I must

There was a stunned silence as Stan finished reading. Suddenly, Addison covered her mouth with her hand.

"Oh my God! Now it makes sense." Her three friends looked at her expectantly. "Do you remember when I went off to the room with the big furnace after we found Stan?"

"Yeah. You said you were being led there by a young girl," Levi said.

"That's right. With everything that happened, I never got a chance to tell you what I saw." She visibly shivered, but forced herself to continue as she described her vision to them. When she was done, Stan gasped aloud.

"Holy crap. Between what you saw and what this journal says…" He shoved his hand through his hair, leaving his bangs standing on end. He suddenly felt Sasha jab him with her elbow.

"Well you dope, don't keep us in suspense."

"It's pretty obvious this Gerald dude is the guy you saw in your visions," he said, pointing to Addison. "One of the articles I found on the internet said that a very dominant spirit can keep other spirits enslaved. It's like the power of their personality keeps other souls from moving on. I bet that's what Gerald did. That's why that place is so haunted. The patients can't move on because he won't let them move on."

"But what about what happened on Halloween back in 1975?" Levi asked. "According to Dr. Fisher, there was a riot."

"Gerald was in a position of authority. Even Fisher admits he should have been more vigilant. Because he wasn't, Gerald could do whatever he wanted. He was telling Fisher that patients were running away. But you saw what really happened, Addison. He was killing them and cremating the bodies so they'd never be found."

"God," Addison whispered.

"The patients finally reached a breaking point. Maybe they finally realized what he was doing and that's what started the riot. They managed to grab Gerald and got their revenge."

"I just realized something," Levi said. "Fisher says he witnessed them killing Gerald under his window. Do you remember what he wrote? Fisher saw them drive a stake through Gerald's chest." He looked at each of them. "It's the same way the German investigator and Devon died. In their case, it was an iron rod through the chest."

"We still don't know why Gerald did it though," Sasha said.

"We may never know."

Suddenly, Sasha turned back to her phone, her fingers flying over the keys. "Damn, where is it?" she muttered to herself. "Ah, here it is." She turned to the others. "Do you remember that article I found when the van driver told us we were going to Meadowlark? It said there had been several disappearances, starting in 1969, in and around Ashboro. At first they thought a serial killer was at work. But they stopped in 1972. What if it was Gerald who was killing people in town? Fisher said there were two orderlies hired in 1969. What if Gerald was one of them? When it got too hot to continue offing people in Ashboro, he turned to the most vulnerable people he could find – the patients in the asylum."

Addison visibly shivered. "I just got a chill on that."

"What does that mean?"

"Aunt Juliette says everything is made up of energy. Even our words and intentions are energy. When an intention lines up with a truth, we get a chill. She calls it the truth chill. I just got one when you mentioned your theory, Sasha."

"I wonder if Dr. Fisher escaped?" Levi replied.

Addison shook her head. "He didn't. I don't know how I know, but I do. He never made it out of his office alive."

"But at least he had time enough to hide the journal in the wall before the patients broke through his door," Stan replied. She nodded. "He wanted the truth to get out."

"Gerald Harper was Ashboro's and Meadowbrook's serial killer," Sasha said. "He killed because he liked to kill. And being dead didn't stop him from continuing to kill."

"One of the articles I read had a saying that I haven't forgotten," Stan spoke up. "Drama in life equals drama in death. In other words, your personality stays with you when you die. If you were in asshole in life, you're going to be an asshole in death until you cross over into the light. Obviously

Gerald was such a dark person, he never ascended into the light. He sure as shit isn't remorseful in any way for what he did. He's continuing to wreak havoc as a malevolent spirit. He really is the Monster of the Asylum."

Sasha sat back with a sigh. "Well, looks like we solved the mystery of Meadowlark. It's too bad no one's ever going to know about it."

"We know about it. Hopefully that's enough to free those souls," Stan said.

"The best thing they can do is tear that place down. Without the building to hold their spirits in place, maybe they can finally move on," Sasha explained. "Especially Gerald Harper. Can you imagine making that place into condos? Gerald will have a friggin' field day terrorizing the condo owners!" She paused for a moment, then said, "Let's talk about something a bit more pleasant." She rubbed her hands gleefully. "What are we going to do with the money the network gave us? Mom's been able to pay off our debt, put a chunk of it into a college fund for me and leave me the leftovers to buy myself a car that won't die every few miles."

"Mine's also going into a college fund for Kylie and myself," Addison spoke up.

"Me too. Though I overheard Dad talking to Mom about taking the family on an RV trip throughout the West next summer. He loves Westerns and has been dying to see Monument Valley and the Grand Canyon," Levi explained.

"How about you?" Addison asked Stan. "What are you going to do?"

"College fund, of course. But," he added with a twinkle in his eye. "I managed to talk my Mom and Dad into giving me a few thousand to do what I like with it."

"They don't know the real reason the network gave us the money, do they?" Addison asked.

Stan shook his head. "No way would I ever tell Mom and Dad it was a payoff cos Devon tried to liquidate me. I told them it was for the pain and suffering we went through when the shit – er – poor guy had his accident." He looked at each of them.

"Great minds think alike," Sasha laughed. "That's pretty much what I told my mother."

Addison and Levi nodded as well.

"Anyway," Stan continued. "I've been looking into buying some state-of-the-art equipment for the Ghost Seekers. After all, if I'm going to remain as the technical expert, I need to have only the best."

Levi threw him a dubious look. "Bro, after all we've been through, you *still* want to do investigations?"

"Definitely. Although working with the Ghost Dudes ended up in a way we never expected, we did get irrefutable proof there is life after death. Aren't you the least bit curious to continue the discovery of why ghosts exist? And if there's any way we can help them to move on to the next plane of existence?" Addison, Sasha and Levi looked at each other. "Look Addy, I know it was tough what you went through. But you gotta admit, you really did connect with the Other Side. Your gifts are amazing!"

"I suppose," she answered warily.

"The more we understand the Other Side, the more we can help you get a handle on what you experience. You know your abilities aren't going to go away any time soon. Forewarned is forearmed."

"Huh?" Levi asked.

Stan rolled his eyes. "If you know about something before it happens, you're better prepared to deal with it."

"I suppose..." she repeated.

"Come on! We're like the four musketeers. One for all and all for one." He smiled warmly at her. "We always have each other's back, right?"

It took her a moment, but she smiled back at him. "Yes, we do."

They all did a palm slap.

"Alright!" Sasha exclaimed. "Watch out ghosts! Addison, Sasha, Levi—" she paused and grinned at Stan, "—and Razor are back in business!"

THE END

AUTHORS' NOTE

J.S. Stephens

Thank you for taking the time to read this book.

For as far back as I can remember, I have communicated with the dead. At the age of fifteen, I was introduced to a woman who studied with Laurie Cabot, the official Witch of Salem, Massachusetts. She took me under her wing and taught me how to work with energy. How to protect myself. And, well, to truly understand and accept the gifts I was given.

For the past twenty years, I've worked as the lead psychic/medium for *The New England Ghost Project,* as well as the former co-host of the popular *Ghost Chronicles* radio show. I've been fortunate enough to have also starred in the Emmy-winning *American Builder* Halloween special. Such an amazing experience!

And, as an FYI, while this book is fiction, it is also based in fact. Both myself and my BFF Bety (aka B.T. Lord) have weaved many of our own experiences into this first book of The Ghost Seekers series.

In the Monster of the Asylum book, you were introduced to Addison, the psychic of the group. Like myself, Addison becomes aware of her abilities at a very young age. It's not all as glorious as it seems. Sure, being a Medium is a blessing, but the gift also carries with it a heavy burden. One that you will experience throughout this series as you walk hand in hand with Addison, Sasha, Levi and Razor investigating things that go bump in the night. And just maybe, if you're lucky, you can pick up a tip or two. Speaking of tips, I have one for you and it's listed below:

Feeling safe and protected:

Protection comes in many forms. Most importantly is holding the intention that you are safe and protected. Grounding the energy is also very important (Bety will be imparting her wisdom on this topic, so make sure to read her author's note too!)

While being strong in yourself and knowing you are safe is important, there may be times when you feel the need to use additional forms of protection. I like to think of it as peeling an onion. The protection being the layers which would need to be peeled away to get to little ol' me.

For instance, when I investigate, if I'm tired or just not feeling myself, I have been known to use the following items for protection: The St. Michael's prayer card, Rosary beads, holy water, coins in my pockets and an array of crystals/metaphysical stones. In fact, if you remember in the story, Aunt Juliette comes to Addison's rescue by creating a crystal grid on her kitchen table and reciting the St. Michael's prayer.

We truly hope you've enjoyed The Monster in the Asylum as much as we have enjoyed writing it. And, we certainly hope you are as eager to journey along with The Ghost Seekers on their next spooky adventure, when you read The Girl Who Died Twice.

If you'd like to find out more about me, or contact me, you can go to my website www.maureen-wood.com

I'm on Facebook under J.S. Stephens-writer.

You can also email me at jsstephenswriter@gmail.com

I love hearing from you and I always respond.

Until next time, be well!

B.T. Lord

As my partner-in-crime J.S. Stephens said, thank you for following the adventures of The Ghost Seekers. We had a great time writing it and we hope you had just as much fun reading it.

Like her, I grew up seeing ghosts. And was part of a paranormal investigation team for many years. As we continue writing this series, we'll be using experiences we really went through encountering the Other Side, as well as adding tips in the Authors' Notes we learned along the way when it comes to dealing, not only with the paranormal, but in everyday life.

I'm fascinated by the paranormal and have spent years studying different belief systems in an effort to make sense of it all. The one that I eventually settled on, because it felt the most right to me, was the study of shamanism. And in particular, the study of energy.

Why energy?

Because everything is made up of energy. And energy has a vibration to it. I can explain it this way: when you're having a bad day, or you're feeling sad or angry or just off, you feel crappy, don't you? Sometimes it's like you can't get out of your own way. That's because you're stuck in what we call lower vibrational energy. Now, when you're having a good day – everything is going great, or better yet, if you feel love for someone or something, you feel fantastic, don't you? That's because you're feeling a high vibrational energy. You feel you can fly, as opposed to feeling a lower vibrational energy, which makes you feel like you're walking through mud.

There may be some of you reading this who feel EVERYTHING. By that I mean, you can't go into a crowded place because you feel overwhelmed. Or you instantly know when your best friend is having a bad day – not because they tell you – but because you can physically *feel* it. Have you ever had the experience of walking up to someone and suddenly feeling a pain in your chest, or in your stomach and you can't figure out why? There's a name for people like you. It's called being an Empath. Empaths are human sponges who soak up the emotions of everyone around them.

So what do you do with all that heavy emotion? If you hold onto it, it drains you. It makes you not want to go out. It makes you want to scream sometimes, doesn't it?

There is a technique called grounding that helps move all that heavy energy out of you. I've been doing it for years – I've taught hundreds of people to do it and let me tell you – it does work. And the best thing is that it's sooooo easy to do. So how do you ground?

Close your eyes and imagine a round red ball about a foot beneath the soles of your feet. Your intention will be to move out any yucky energy or heavy emotions you're feeling into that red ball. Remember, energy follows intention. In other words, if you label energy as bad, your intention is that it's going to be bad. And guess what? It's going to be bad. If you label energy as good, your intention is that it's going to be good. And it will be good. In truth, energy is just energy until you decide what it's going to be – low vibration or high vibration – bad or good. When you ground, remember that you're intending to feel better – to move all that crummy energy out of you so you can get back to feeling good.

Therefore, focus your attention on this red ball. The more you focus on this ball, the more you should begin to feel your emotions slowly moving from your head, down through your chest and stomach, slowly oozing down your abdomen and legs and out the bottom of your feet into this ball. You may feel your feet tingling and you will begin to feel lighter the more you do this.

Now if the emotions you're feeling are in your stomach, you can bring the red ball up into your belly, and picture it moving in a circle. As it spins around, it's gathering all that heavy emotion that's making you feel heavy. After a few moments, the ball should start to slow down. When it does, picture it moving back down your legs, your feet and into the ground.

That's pretty simple, isn't it?

Be sure to let me know how it works for you.

Now, a word about my other books. If you like murder mysteries, try my series, The Twin Ponds Mysteries. They're set in a small town in the wilderness of Maine where some pretty interesting things take place that Sheriff Cammie Farnsworth and her team must solve.

If you like murder mysteries with a paranormal twist, check out my Coffin Islands Paranormal Mysteries. They're set on a group of islands located out in the ocean two hours from Portland, Maine. They're cursed, so you can imagine all the creepy stuff that happens there.

Both series can be found on Amazon.

I also offer a free mystery novella, set during Halloween, on my website www.btlordwriter.com

It features the characters from Twin Ponds, and it has a paranormal twist to it. All you need to do is sign up for my newsletter, which I only use to let you know when I have a new book coming out.

You can drop me a line at btlordwriter@gmail.com or on my Facebook page

https://www.facebook.com/BTLordWriter/

I love hearing from you and I always respond.

If you're interested in learning more about the gift of empathy, I have a series of books, written under my real name Bety Comerford –with my writing partner Steve Wilson - that goes deeper into what being an empath is all about. The first book in the series is the award-winning *The Reluctant Empath*. It's been helping empaths all over the world and I'm sure it will help you as well.

In the meantime, we've included an excerpt from Book 2 in the Ghost Seekers Paranormal Mysteries. It's called The Girl Who Died Twice and it will be out in late summer of 2019.

Enjoy!

Preview of Book 2 in
The Ghost Seekers Paranormal
Mysteries

***

THE GIRL WHO DIED TWICE

***

Available late
Summer 2019

PROLOGUE

Early December

Sixteen year old Addison Monroe sat at her bedroom window, looking out over her front yard. Just that morning, she, her twelve-year-old sister Kylie and her mother had spent a few hours putting up the Christmas decorations. Snow was forecast that evening and Anne Monroe wanted to make sure the lights and plastic figures of Santa, his reindeer and elves were up and ready to be lit at the first sign of dusk.

Although this was her favorite time of year, and she always looked forward to it, this holiday season found the teenager feeling a bit down in the dumps.

That past summer, she, along with her best friends, Sasha Marquez, Levi Taylor and Stan (aka Razor) Crane, had been chosen over thousands of paranormal investigative teams to join the famous The Ghost Dudes on their television show. The live broadcast of their investigation was to take place on Halloween night at one of America's most haunted locations.

The location turned out to be the Meadowlark Mental Asylum, located just over one hour from where Addison and her friends lived. Rumors had abounded for years that the building, built in 1869, was inhabited by an evil presence known as The Monster of the Asylum. It had been abruptly closed down in 1975, the reasons buried and forgotten.

Calling themselves The Ghost Seekers, Sasha, Levi and Stan had been excited to be appearing on television next to a group of seasoned investigators they'd been watching for two years. It was Addison who'd gone into the venture with nervous unease. She'd been designated the group psychic and during the night inside the asylum, she'd been forced to confront the fact that she did have abilities she could no longer ignore.

She would never forget what they'd experienced in the malevolent location. Nor the fact that they'd all been lucky to escape, not only with their lives, but with their sanity.

The memories of the horrors they'd undergone still lingered in Addison's psyche, giving rise to the occasional nightmare that brought it all crashing back. She'd tried to make sense of it all, including the undeniable fact that as much as she didn't want to admit it, she was a psychic, with the uncanny ability to communicate with the dead.

It didn't help that admitting her so-called gifts was a very sore point in her family, particularly with her mother. Anne and her twin sister Juliette had grown up living with frequent interaction with ghosts. Terrified, Anne had completely turned away from it, convinced the encounters were nothing more than the results from her overactive imagination. This adamant belief was reinforced by her mother, who also feared their sensitivities. Juliette, on the other hand, fully embraced her gifts and now supplemented her income as an artist by giving readings and healings to others.

Because of Anne's refusal to acknowledge the existence of a sixth sense that run in the family lineage, it left her relationship with Juliette in tatters. A victim of the broken relationship was Addison. Feeling and seeing things she couldn't understand, she was unable to go to her mother for guidance. Yet, if she approached her aunt, her mother would go ballistic. She had no choice but to secretly reach out to Juliette to help make sense of what she'd been through, especially in the Meadowlark Asylum.

As Razor reminded her, her gifts weren't going away any time soon. It was important she find someone she could trust to explain what being psychic was all about.

She couldn't think of anyone she trusted more than her Aunt Juliette.

But not even Juliette could help with her growing depression. She tried to tell herself she was feeling blue because of her experiences at Meadowlark. But it was deeper than that. In those moments of honest clarity, she couldn't run away from the fact that she wasn't sure she wanted to be psychic. It was too much responsibility. She wanted to be what she considered 'normal'. She wanted to be like her friends who never had to worry about having ghosts popping up at the end of their beds, or seeing the images of long dead pets still sitting on her pillow at night.

"I'm sorry, baby, but these gifts, once given, are not taken away. You simply need to learn how to navigate them," Juliette told her.

"But Mom's turned them off. You told me you two grew up seeing ghosts all the time, yet she never sees anything anymore."

Juliette turned a knowing eye to her niece. "Just because she doesn't mention it, doesn't mean it's still not happening."

So there she was. Stuck between a rock and a hard place. She had gifts she wasn't sure she wanted, yet at the same time was intrigued by her abilities.

What a mess.

Maybe she should just shelve her worries. Wallowing in it wasn't going to change anything anytime soon. Besides, Christmas was in a few weeks. She'd hate herself for allowing her sad mood to ruin it, not only for herself, but for her family.

"It is what it is," Addison whispered under her breath, borrowing one of Razor's favorite sayings.

She smiled slightly. She was still getting used to calling Stan 'Razor'. He'd insisted upon it when they'd first approached him to join The Ghost Seekers last summer, but he hadn't truly earned the nickname until the events at

Meadowlark. Even Sasha, who could be a hard ass about such things, was now calling him Razor.

At least it made him happy. And at this time of year, everyone deserved to be happy.

Even her.

It was almost dusk and the Christmas decorations from the surrounding houses were slowly coming to life. As Addison waited for theirs to come on, she turned her attention to the huge inflated Santa in the middle of the lawn she and her mother had struggled to put up. Kylie had burst out in hysterical laughter as Anne, laboring to get the huge blown up figure positioned just right, somehow fell onto Santa's stomach. Even Addison had found it funny, though she'd tried not to laugh out loud as her mother floundered to free herself from the air filled limbs.

Hoping to see the row of candy canes they'd placed along the driveway come on, Addison was surprised to see a young girl standing there. She hadn't been there a moment before, yet there she stood, staring right up at Addison.

The light was fading and it was difficult to clearly discern the girl's face, but there was something about her that looked very familiar. Addison stood up and pulled open her window. She was immediately struck by a blast of cold, winter air that sent shivers throughout her body. If she was smart, she'd close the window before she got sick, and ignore whoever was standing out there. Yet, she couldn't. Propelled by curiosity and a sense that she needed to know who this girl was and, more importantly, why she remained staring up at Addison on such a frigid night, she leaned out the window and peered down at the figure.

The girl was very still as her head remained tilted up towards Addison's second floor bedroom. A breeze came up and ruffled her shoulder length black hair, sending its tendrils up into her face. But she didn't brush it away. She remained motionless, as if she were frozen to the spot.

Addison was about to call down to her, to ask what she wanted, when a memory burst into her consciousness. She gasped aloud as she stared down at the girl in shock and recognition. Then, in one swift movement, she ducked back inside, slammed the window closed and backed away until she fell onto her bed.

It couldn't be true. It was impossible.

But the more she tried to reason it away, the more she realized she hadn't been hallucinating. She knew what she saw. And who she saw.

It was her sister's best friend, Becca Fraser.

Who died two years ago.

Made in the USA
Monee, IL
16 March 2020